The Twisted Menora
and other
Devora Doresh Mysteries

by

Carol Korb Hubner

Illustrated by

G. A. Morganroth

Judaica Press • 1987
New York

Contents

Contents

The Twisted Menora

And for homework I want each of you to write an essay about what the Chanukah lights mean to you. Yesterday we spoke about what *ChaZaL* say, and I expect you to incorporate some of that in your essay. . . ."

The class groaned in unison. Shaindy turned to Devora and whispered: "The only reason we have Chanukah vacation is to have enough time to do all the homework they dream up for us!" Devora nodded sympathetically and turned back to the teacher. Morah Chana had a resigned expression on her face.

"That's enough, girls! The assignment will be easy to do—you have eight nights of candle lighting to think about it."

Just then the bell rang, and the girls got up to leave, chattering as they packed their books into their bags. Morah Chana sighed. It was impossible to get any work done the day before vacation when these kids were so restless.

Devora and Shaindy walked out of the school building together. Devora turned to her friend and smiled mysteriously. "Guess what?"

Shaindy tossed her long brown hair and looked expectantly at Devora. "What?"

"This morning, before I left for school, my father got a phone call from Yossi—the *bochur* who used to stay at our house for *Shabbos* while he was attending yeshiva. Yossi told my father that his fiance broke their engagement, and he's very upset about it. He didn't exactly say what happened, but he has invited us to come up to Massachusetts for the weekend! And my father said yes! We're leaving this afternoon!

Shaindy looked at her friend, her eyes wide, "Massachusetts! You're so lucky!" Suddenly Shaindy's face fell. "Oh—but we promised Shulamith and Rochel that we'd go ice skating with them on Monday. Will you be home in time?"

Devora shrugged. "I guess so. My mother said we'd be back on Monday morning."

They had reached Shaindy's house, and Shaindy was looking up at the house grimly.

"I have to watch my sister again. I never have any time to myself. She's such a pain!"

"I think the same thing about Chaim most of the time. His newest thing is trying out for the Yeshiva chorus. He's constantly playing those Aharon ben Avraham records at full blast, and it's driving us all crazy. Even *I* know the words by heart already! But then I think about how great it will be when we all grow up."

"Yeah. I guess so. Enjoy your trip—and don't get involved in any detective cases. See you Monday."

"*Chag Sameach.*"

Devora skipped down the block to her house. She hadn't realized how excited she really was until just now. Wouldn't it be wonderful if it were snowing in Massachusetts! She ran up the front steps, and headed straight for the kitchen. She threw her books on the table, and shouted upstairs.

"Hello! Mom! Are you home?"

"Is that you, Devora? I'm upstairs. Don't take too long in the kitchen—you have to hurry up and pack. Abba will be home in half an hour and he wants us to be ready to leave."

"Okay," said Devora, opening the refrigerator door, "I'm just getting something to eat."

She stood in front of the open refrigerator staring at its contents. She decided to have raspberry yogurt and a glass of orange juice. Devora brought lunch up to her room and packed between spoonfuls. Finally, reaching into the drawer of her desk, she pulled out a large leather bag. Last week, for her birthday, her friends had presented her with a detective set. It had a real finger-printing set as well as a survival kit, with a collapsible knife, fork and spoon, a flashlight and a screwdriver on a keychain, and—best of all—a set of business cards with her name and phone number printed on them. Now she was practically a *professional!*

Mrs. Doresh was in her bedroom finishing up the packing. Everything was already such a rush, she thought. Luckily the children had only a half day of school today so that they could leave before dark.

"I'm ready," said Devora, standing at her mother's bedroom door, grinning. "So am I," said Mrs. Doresh, "if I could only close this suitcase."

Devora sat on the overstuffed suitcase while her mother fastened the latches. They carried the suitcases down the stairs and left them in front of the door. Devora thought she heard a car pull up, and stuck her head out of the door to see who was coming.

"Abba's here!" said Devora.

Rebbe Doresh walked into the house with Chaim. Rebbe Doresh was tall and handsome, with a neatly trimmed beard and a booming voice.

"Is everyone ready?"

"Almost, dear. If you would pack the Chanukah menora and the oil for me, I think we'll be done," answered Mrs. Doresh.

Chaim ran up the stairs towards his bedroom and came down clutching a large bag.

"Devora! Look how many *dreidels* I have!"

Devora stood in front of a large mirror in the hallway, fixing her hair.

"You must be the luckiest boy in the world, Chaim. I sure am jealous," she said sarcastically.

Chaim glared at his older sister.

"You think you're such a big deal. I'm not even going to let you play with them!"

"What makes you think I want to play dreidel with you?" snarled Devora.

"Children! I don't want to hear a single fight between the two of you all weekend. Let's see if you can maintain a cease-fire for *one* weekend!"

Rebbe Doresh entered the room with an exquisite silver menora wrapped in plastic. "Let's not forget the family menora," said Rebbe Doresh. "I think we're ready to put these suitcases in the car, and we'll be on our way."

"Wait" said Chaim "I'm taking my menora too." In his hand he held an old brass menora that was chipped and scarred.

"Are you kidding?" asked Devora. "I didn't know you still had it!"

"After all, it saved my life once," he sniffed, holding it protectively.

Devora shrugged and said nothing. She remembered how her brother had come home one wintry evening with that menora. A bully had started up with him on his way home from school. The bigger boy had thrown Chaim into the snow and had pounced on him. Suddenly Chaim felt this metal pipe under the snow and he used it as leverage against the boy on top of him. The bully fell off of him and Chaim got up and ran away. When he got home, he realized that he still held the pipe in his hands except that it wasn't a pipe . . . it was a menora. He kept the menora as a momento that Hashem watches over us all the time. This Chanukah, like the previous one, he wanted his menora with him.

"I took along the tapes of the Chanukah choir," said Devora. "We can play them on the car stereo while we drive."

"Do you have my solo?" asked Chaim, pleased with the idea of hearing himself singing all the way to Boston.

"No, just the choir."

As he opened his eyes wide in protest, Mrs. Doresh turned around and frowned.

"That wasn't necessary, Devora."

"But I like the way his eyes get big when he's angry!"

"I don't care. You are not allowed to enjoy yourself at someone else's expense—especially if it's your brother."

"She always starts up with me," sulked Chaim.

"Baby's gonna cry!" shot back Devora.

"See what I mean?"

"Enough of this!" Rebbe Doresh pulled the car over to the side of the road and stopped. "I don't want to hear any more of this squabbling. If you have nothing nice to say to each other, don't say anything at all. At least then your mother and I can enjoy some peace and quiet on our way to Yossi's."

Devora and her brother nodded and remained silent as their father edged the car back into traffic. After a few minutes Devora took the Chanukah tape and asked her father to play it.

"I think your solo was beautiful," she said quietly to Chaim.

Chaim smiled at his sister.

"Yeah," he said brightly. "So do I."

"I hope we can be of some comfort to Yossi," said Rebbe Doresh. "He sounded so upset when I spoke to him on the phone. So don't pester Yossi with a lot of questions, children. Wait until he decides to talk about it, alright?"

Her father sounded almost as upset as Yossi must be, thought Devora. Yossi Feld had been Rebbe Doresh's student, and a warm friendship had developed between them. Until he decided to leave the yeshiva in New York, Yossi had spent every Shabbos at the Doreshes' home and they had gotten to know each other well.

As a young boy Yossi had struggled with his family

to be able to learn in a Yeshiva, to keep the Sabbath and the laws of *kashruth*. Now, with his love of Torah, he decided that the time had come for him to go out into small communities and teach others what he had been lucky enough to learn as a child.

Yossi was now working on a college campus giving lectures and trying to teach Jewish students about their heritage. He had been having a great deal of success with the students there, but his efforts were being counteracted by a cult that had recently appeared on campus. The last time Yossi had visited the Doreshes, he had sounded distinctly worried. The group, called Bnei Shem, was led by a man under investigation by the F.B.I.

Devora leaned forward in her seat, addressing her mother.

"Why did Mina break off their engagement?"

Mrs. Doresh shrugged her shoulders. "Devora, sometimes these things happen. I really don't know why. And neither does Yossi, I'm afraid. This is one mystery that even you can't solve."

Chaim began to get restless.

"We'll be there in 10 minutes or so," said Rebbe Doresh. Suddenly they heard a bang and the car began to wobble. "Oh no . . . I hope we don't have a flat . . ."

But they did. They all got out of the car while Rebbe Doresh opened the trunk and took out the jack. Chaim put his menora next to a tree and began playing with his ball. It didn't take long for Rebbe Doresh to change the tire and soon everyone was summoned back into the car. As the car pulled back onto the road, Chaim shouted: "Stop . . . I left my Menora back there!"

Rebbe Doresh stopped the car as Chaim explained in tears, "I got out of the car with my ball and my Menora. I left the Menora near a tree while I played. When you told us to get back into the car, I did . . . but I forgot my menora."

Rebbe Doresh turned the car around and drove back to the spot where he had fixed the flat. Chaim ran over to the tree . . . but the Menora was gone.

He felt devastated.

"Don't cry, Chaim," Devora tried to console him, "Whoever found your Menora . . . I am sure . . . will find it as lucky as you did."

"You think so?" He stopped crying and wiped away a tear.

Devora smiled and nodded her head.

It was getting dark when the Doreshes arrived in Peabody, the small town in New England where Yossi lived. As they drew up in front of Yossi's house, a young man ran out to meet them. It was Yossi, looking pale and drawn, but nevertheless happy to see them.

When they finished unloading the car, Yossi showed them around his home. It had taken him a long time to find it. He had furnished it with care, and now he was very proud of it.

"Wow! This is the most beautiful house I've ever seen!" exclaimed Devora as she walked into the living room. "When I get married, I'll furnish my place exactly like this. Are those antiques?"

Yossi grinned at Devora and nodded.

"Not all of them. Some of this stuff is just used furniture. Mina's father had an antique store, and when he died last year Mina had a big sale to get rid of the inventory. I had always loved antiques, but could never afford them. Anyway, that's where I met Mina." Yossi leaned against an old oak bookcase, and looked down at the floor uncomfortably.

Rebbe Doresh looked sympathetically at his friend and changed the subject.

"It is late, Yossele. Where is the shul here? It's time to *daven*."

"There is a shul only a few blocks from here. Wait until I put supper in the oven, and we'll walk together."

Mrs. Doresh turned to Yossi in surprise. "You made supper? Since when do you know how to cook?"

"I got tired of eating out all the time. I bought some pots and pans and a cookbook, and have gotten quite good at it. You'll have a chance to judge for yourself at dinner."

After he took two casserole dishes from the refrigerator and placed them in the oven, he turned back to Rebbe Doresh and motioned to the door. As the two men, accompanied by Chaim, left to go to shul, Devora and her mother began to set the table. When the men returned, the family washed, recited the *bracha* over the bread, and sat down to dinner.

"Mmm! This is really good, Yossi," exclaimed Chaim. "I didn't know you could cook so well."

Yossi beamed, and Mrs. Doresh glanced at her husband.

"Well, maybe Yossi can teach Abba, Chaim," she said.

Rebbe Doresh smiled and quickly changed the subject. He asked Yossi about the coffee house he had started on the college campus.

"It's really doing much better than it was the last time I spoke to you. I think we're finally getting it off the ground. It's very important that it be successful. There are so many Jewish students at the university who are away from home for the first time. When they're lonely, they're an easy target for that new missionary group, Bnei Shem."

"But don't they know that they're Jewish?" asked Chaim.

"Unfortunately, not many of them do. Some of them come from homes where the only religion is a faith in material goods. How wrong are they to reject a religion they believe to be nothing more than eating Gefilte fish?"

"But that's like saying that you're Italian because you eat pizza!" said Devora. "Can't anything be done?"

"It's the parents as well as the children who have to be educated. Many uneducated Jewish parents think that Judaism is archaic. And besides, their child wasn't going to be a rabbi so he or she didn't need to go to Hebrew School. But their children learn math, and they're not mathematicians . . . they learn music and they're not musicians. Why can't they learn Torah and not be rabbis?"

Mrs. Doresh was shaking her head sadly. "Exactly what do *you* do about this, Yossi?"

"I talk to them a lot. I try to make them see what beautiful traditions we have, and that the Torah has kept us alive for thousands of years. I try to tell them how many oppressors have tried to destroy us physically but the Jewish people have managed to survive. In our days, through assimilation and intermarriage we are destroying ourselves spiritually.

"At first we didn't have a great deal of success. But then I decided to offer classes in Jewish history, Jewish holidays, Israeli folk dance, Jewish mysticism, and Hebrew calligraphy. After that, we really had our hands full. Mina was teaching the class in calligraphy.

She really is very good at it . . ." Yossi's voice trailed off and he looked unhappily at his guests.

"I guess I should tell you what happened." He cleared his throat.

"Yesterday I went to City Hall to do some research on a shul that is on Mina's property. When I came back to the house, I telephoned Mina. There appeared to be trouble on the line, so I called the operator. She said that the line had been disconnected! Why should Mina disconnect the phone? Her mother and her father have both passed away, and she lives alone—well, I was very worried. I got in the car and drove over to her house. I was even more worried after I rang the doorbell, because a strange man answered the door! He was very strange looking; completely bald with incredibly bushy black eyebrows. I told him who I was, and demanded to see Mina. He refused to let me in—he said that Mina wasn't home.

"From the doorway, I could see a woman sitting on the couch in the living room. I pushed my way in the door past the stranger. She had short hair and a faraway look in her eyes. She looked like Mina, but when she looked up, she appeared not to see me at all! It was as if she didn't know me. When I asked her about the phone, she said that she had decided to change the phone number. I was stunned by the whole thing, and as I was standing there, thinking about what I could say to bring her back to normal, she suddenly glared at me and shouted: 'The engagement is off. I never want to see you again!'" Yossi paused, a pained look in his eyes. He took a deep breath as if to steady himself, and began again.

"When I finally understood what she said, I asked her what had happened. She looked surprised and replied that nothing had happened. 'I just changed my mind, that's all. I never want to see you again,' she said. Rebbe Doresh, she wasn't even looking at me! Then, without turning around, she said very quietly, 'Please don't make a scene. Go now.' I didn't know what else to do . . . so I left.

"I'm still in shock. I've never seen her like that before. We were always totally honest with each other . . . it's impossible for a person to change so quickly." Yossi shook his head in bewilderment, and gulped down some soda. His thin, wiry body drooped sadly.

Rebbe Doresh leaned back in his chair and stroked his beard thoughtfully. He looked at Yossi with compassion.

"It does sound rather strange. Did you have some kind of disagreement?"

Yossi shook his head.

"How was she acting the last time you saw her?"

Yossi thought a moment before replying. "The last time I saw here was late on Monday. She had taught the calligraphy class in the afternoon. Afterwards she took some of her students home with her for coffee, and I went along. When they were looking at her work and browsing through some of her books on calligraphy, I remembered something I had promised to show her—a copy of a medieval *Ketuba*.

"I left by her back door and took a shortcut through the woods that adjoin her property. It was already dark, and I must have taken a wrong turn, because I was suddenly in a clearing I had never seen before. There was an old wooden building in front of me. I was really surprised—I thought I knew the woods so well! When I went closer to examine it, I was even more surprised. Over the doorway, there was a carving of two lions facing each other, holding a *Magen David* between them. I guess the building used to be a shul of some kind. The name "Solomon" was carved on the right hand side of the door, with the number 1829. That must be the year it was built."

Chaim leaned forward excitedly. "Wow! A secret building? Did you go in?"

Yossi was too lost in thought to even notice the interruption. "I tried the door—the hinges were rusty, but I was able to push it open. Inside, the building was dusty and full of cobwebs. There was one large room, with an ornately carved wooden *bima* in the middle of it. A few old pews were scattered around, and all the windows had been boarded up. A second, smaller room housed a large wooden menora that was twisted and broken. I was curious to see what kind of shul this was, and looked around for some *chumashim* or *siddurim*—they sometimes write the name of the congregation on the flyleaf. I couldn't find any, but that's not to say that there isn't a *geniza* hidden somewhere."

Noticing the puzzled look on Devora's face, Rebbe Doresh explained, "In earlier days the synagogue was usually the focal point of a community, so that books, letters, and important documents were stored there. Old *seforim,* some we didn't even know existed, have turned up in the *geniza* of old shuls about to be destroyed. Sometimes actual scrolls have turned up. Don't you remember I mentioned the Cairo Geniza to you once? The one found by Solomon Schecter in 1890?"

Devora nodded.

"Finish your story, Yossi," Mrs. Doresh urged.

"It was getting darker and darker out, and I was afraid that maybe I was really lost, so I ran back to the woods, found the path, and hurried home. When I got back to Mina's I told her about my great find. She wasn't even surprised! It turns out that the building belongs to her! Her great-grandfather came to Massachusetts from Spain in the early part of the nineteenth century. He had been a Rabbi in Europe, and many of his congregants followed him to America. They built this shul on the back of his property, and it was used for more than one hundred years. I guess as more and more Jews moved away from town it fell into disuse, and Mina's father had closed the building. Mina had no idea where the *sefer torah* or *siddurim* are hidden."

Yossi poured himself more soda. "The story doesn't end there. When Mina was sixteen, her mother suddenly became ill and died. She had a sister, a year younger, who was very upset by the tragedy and ran away from home. She had been hanging around with the wrong group of kids. Mr. Solomon was very distraught, to say the least."

"What ever happened to Mina's sister?" inquired Devora.

"She seems to have disappeared from the face of the earth. Mr. Solomon tried everything—even private detectives—but to no avail. Not knowing his younger daughter's whereabouts, Mr. Solomon left all of his property to Mina. Poor wayward kid, I wonder what has happened to her . . ." Yossi's voice broke off as a lump formed in his throat.

"What is really upsetting is that Mina told me that night that she was thinking about fixing up the shul and re-opening it. That was going to be her surprise for me." Yossi turned to Rebbe Doresh and shrugged. "That was the last time I spoke to her. I have no idea

what happened to her in the two days between now
and then." His eyes glistened with unshed tears.

The family was silent for several minutes after Yossi
finished speaking. Life sure is complicated when you are
grown up, Devora thought. Why would Mina break
her engagement? She had no family, and Yossi was surely a wonderful man. And what was to become of the
old shul that was hers? This was quite a puzzle. So many
missing pieces, too. Suddenly she had an idea.

"Yossi, do you think we can go see this shul?"

"Sure, I don't see why not. After all, it is public
property." Yossi turned to his teacher and friend.
"Rebbe Doresh, you'll find the place fascinating."

Rebbe Doresh smiled. "And maybe my detective
daughter will find the *geniza*!"

"Then we'll go tomorrow morning," Yossi decided
as he reached for the *bentschers*.

After *bentsching* Mrs. Doresh rose from the table and
rolled up her sleeves. Yossi immediately stood up and
began to clear the table. Mrs. Doresh smiled.

"Yossi, you made a lovely dinner, now you must let
me clean up. Why don't you and my husband go into
the other room to chat?"

"Please, Mrs. Doresh, you are a guest in my home.
You go into the living room and I'll join you shortly."

"Why, that's very sweet of you, Yossi. Thank you,
But at least let my children help you. Devora, you do

the dishes with Yossi; Chaim, please clear the table."

Chaim groaned loudly and pleaded, "Oh Mom, do I *have* to?"

"Chaim!" said Mrs. Doresh sternly. Chaim knew it was one of those times when she really meant it. Resigning himself to the task, he went about clearing the table.

Early the next morning Yossi drove the Doreshes to the shul. Because there was no road leading directly to it, they had to leave the car and walk through the woods to reach it. He had described the shul perfectly, thought Devora. In the morning light the building looked older and more decrepit than she imagined. Nonetheless, it was beautiful.

As they filed inside the building, Mrs. Doresh headed straight for the *bima*. "Look at how elaborate this carving is! The shul must have been quite a showplace." Four steps led up to the *bima* on either side, and the steps were flanked by banisters.

"It's a wonder this *bima* hasn't been broken," observed Rabbi Doresh. "Especially since those pews look worn and battered."

Yossi nodded. "They certainly do. Now where do you suppose the *geniza* is?" He turned to Devora. "You're the detective among us. Where do *you* think they've hidden the *sefer torah* and *siddurim*?"

Devora's keen blue eyes lit up, intrigued by the challenge. "It would have to be in a place they knew was airtight, so that the parchment and paper would remain intact. Or perhaps they buried them."

"Devora! There's a small cemetery just a few yards from here. It's very old . . . they probably hid the *geniza* there."

"Then let's go! What are we waiting for?"

The Doreshes trooped out after Yossi and followed him to the cemetery. About twelve headstones protruded from the ground. Chaim bounded from stone to stone, reading the name written on each one.

Devora stood lost in thought. They could have constructed a false grave. She examined each of the gravestones for any telltale sign. They all looked authentic. Leaving her family musing about clues hidden in the names, she headed back inside the shul. The *bima* was truly beautiful. Lions and trees were carved into its surface. She ran her hands over the carvings. Perhaps it was hollow? She put her ear to the wood and knocked gently. There was no echo.

Sighing in frustration, Devora walked into the other room. It looked exactly like the first room . . . except it did not have a beautifully carved *bima*. Instead, at the far end of the room stood a large broken Chanukah menora whose branches seemed purposefully twisted out of shape. Devora walked over to the twisted menora and stared at it. It was a shame that the shul was in such disrepair. With a little care, it could be really beautiful. Her fingers reached up and touched one of the menora's hanging branches. She raised it up . . . it seemed to eagerly swing back into its proper place, but when her hand let go, it dropped down again. She studied the menora again. Something bothered her about it, but what? The wind sounded stronger outside and she felt as if the shul was stretching and turning, showing its signs of age. She shivered as she heard it creak on its hinges and she walked over to the window and looked outside. Everyone was coming back from the little cemetery . . . they were laughing at something Chaim had said. Devora stepped out through the front entrance which was the only mutual area between the two rooms (as the wall otherwise divided them) and smiled at her mother.

Mrs. Doresh was looking at her watch nervously. "There you are, Devora. We couldn't figure out where you'd wandered off to. We have to leave now—it's really late and we have to shop and shower before Shabbos."

They walked back to the car and Yossi drove them into town. Peabody was so small it had only one main street, which bore the unimaginative name of Main

Street. Yossi, together with Rebbe and Mrs. Doresh, went into the supermarket. Chaim and Devora were left outside to explore.

After scouting out every store on Main Street, they soon reached the newspaper office. This was the first time Devora had ever seen a place where a newspaper was produced. Walking inside, she whispered to Chaim, "It's just like they describe it in books!" There was a row of messy desks with typewriters on them. Bulletin boards plastered with memos lined the walls. There was no one in the office but a small, middle-aged man with a huge cigar in his mouth.

"Hi there! Can I help you two?"

Devora assumed her most adult voice. "I'd like to see a copy of your newspaper, please."

"Sure thing!" the man said, smiling. He walked to the rear of the office where tied bundles of newspapers were stacked. Grabbing one of the bundles, he removed the string and brought several copies to Devora and Chaim.

"You came just in time. The latest edition is just out. Hot off the presses, as they say."

Devora picked up a newspaper. *The Peabody Press.* It smelled of fresh ink. "Is this a daily or a weekly?"

The man bit down on his cigar and chuckled. "It's a weekly. This is a small town, sweetie. There's not enough happening here to fill up a daily."

At that moment the door to the office opened and a young woman with a bunch of fliers in her hand entered the room. She was tall and slim, with a red kerchief tied tightly around her hair. She might have been pretty were it not for the sullen look on her face. She walked over to the newspaper man and glared at him angrily.

"We printed up our own fliers, thank you very much. Not everyone in this town is as narrow-minded as you are." She waved the stack of fliers in his face. "Why don't you come to our meeting? It might do you some good."

She turned to Chaim and Devora, standing behind her. "Here," she said, handing each of them a flier, "bring your friends."

Devora read the words on the paper she held in her hand. It said "WELCOME TO BNEI SHEM. WE'LL HELP YOU FIND GOD IN YOUR LIFE. Our new headquarters will open in three weeks at the Old Solomon House on Carriage Lane. Refreshments will be served after the opening ceremony."

The woman turned to leave.

"Wait!" yelled Devora. "Is your headquarters Mina Solomon's old shul?"

The woman stared at Devora curiously. "That's right," she said slowly. And then she abruptly turned and left.

The newspaper man had been looking at the flier and was now muttering under his breath. Still chewing his fat cigar, he questioned Devora, "So you know the Solomon girl, do ya?"

"Well, actually I have never met her. She used to be engaged to my father's friend."

"Oh yeah. We announced the engagement in the paper. Big item. The Solomons were among the oldest residents of Peabody. What's her fiance's name?" The man scratched his balding head.

Chaim announced, "Yossi Feld. But the engagement is off."

The newspaperman stared at him a minute before speaking. "So she's turning her property over to Bnei Shem. Another one of those blind cult followers. Her father would turn over in his grave if he knew what was happening. Just as well he didn't live to see this." He shook his head from side to side. "Such a sweet little girl she was, too. And so much trouble in that family. What a shame, what a shame." Chewing violently on his cigar, he looked accusingly at Devora and Chaim. "Crazy kids."

Devora poked Chaim in the ribs.

"Ouch! What are you poking me for?" he complained.

"Why didn't you remind me what time it is? Mommy is going to have our heads!"

Devora dropped some coins on the desk to pay for the newspaper and said a hasty goodbye to the man. Outside, she grabbed Chaim's hand and pulled him down the street.

"Hurry up! Wait until Yossi hears about this!"

The two of them raced back to the supermarket. Rebbe Doresh and Yossi were standing outside with bags of groceries at their feet. Rebbe Doresh looked impatient. Yossi looked worried. Mrs. Doresh came walking out of the pet store, shaking her head.

"There you are! I've been looking for you kids everywhere! Where have you been?" she demanded angrily.

Devora answered breathlessly. "You wouldn't believe what happened, Mommy! We went to look at the newspaper office—we had never seen one—there was a man with a giant cigar there—then this lady came in—she was from one of those missionary groups Yossi told us about—well look, she gave us this flier!" Devora handed the paper to her mother and continued impatiently. "Don't you see? Bnei Shem is taking over the shul!"

Yossi looked aghast and tore the flier from Mrs. Doresh's hand. Staring at it he asked slowly, "What did you say this girl looked like? It sounds a little like Mina—but she'd never wear a kerchief—not before we're married anyway. I can't believe she'd become involved with people like that, she's much too bright. I've got to get to the bottom of this whole mystery— I'm going over there right now."

"Yossele," said Rebbe Doresh quietly, "look at your watch."

"Nuts! It's an hour and a half before Shabbos. There won't be time to get over there and back home before sundown."

Rebbe Doresh picked up the bag of groceries at his feet. "After Shabbos, Yossele, we'll take care of all of this."

The next day at the Shabbos table Devora told her parents about the essay she had to write for Morah Chana.

"That's an interesting assignment, to write about what the Chanukah lights mean to you," Rebbe Doresh remarked. "What will you write, Devora?"

His daughter looked at him thoughtfully. "I haven't really thought about it yet. Things here have been so interesting."

Chaim perked up. "I learned in school that lighting the Chanukah menora should remind us that Hashem is everywhere. Because the miracle of Chanukah is actually a small one compared to the splitting of the Red Sea and things like that." Chaim grinned at his sister with satisfaction.

Rebbe Doresh smiled affectionately at his son. "That's very good, Chaim."

"Yeah, Chaim, it is good. Sometimes you surprise me, little brother. I think that this Chanukah I'm going to rededicate myself to trying to figure you out!"

After this surprising declaration Devora lapsed into silence. She reached for a piece of challah. Sometimes it was good just to chew and think quietly. Maybe something would come to her; maybe the pieces of the puzzle would fit together if she weren't trying so hard to force them in place. She thought back on the events of yesterday: the visit to the newspaper office, the trip to the Solomon shul. Why was there a huge Chanukah menora in this shul? Didn't most shuls have regular menoras with 6 branches?

"Abba, isn't it true that a menora has to have all of its branches in a row? Morah Chana taught us that the menora is *posul* if its branches are twisted. Why does the Solomon shul have a twisted menora? I don't think they are broken at all. Everytime I twisted a branch into position and then let go, it swung naturally back into that odd shape. I think they are twisted on purpose."

"Are you serious?" asked Yossi. "I didn't notice that at all. I just thought it was slightly damaged. Maybe we should take another look at it."

"I bet you the *geniza* is hidden under the menora

after all," said Chaim. "Maybe old Mr. Solomon meant it to be a clue to the whereabouts of the *geniza* . . . to whoever will own the Shul . . . a sign for generations, from one son to the next."

It sounded very dramatic the way Chaim said it and Devora wrinkled her nose. "I think you've got it! By George, you got it!" she laughed.

"You wanta take me on as your partner?" Chaim asked. "Obviously you need someone like me."

Yossi looked suddenly alert. "You know—Chaim, you could be right. Shabbos ends early tonight. First, I'd like to go over to Mina's house. Afterwards we can stop off at the shul and check out the menora."

"Oh please!" Devora exclaimed enthusiastically, looking to her mother for permission. "May I go?"

Mrs. Doresh chuckled. "You're the detective in the family. I don't see how they could go without you."

"Can I go, too?" Chaim whined.

"After all, you're the detective's assistant. I guess I'll have to let you go too."

Chaim's eyes filled with excitement. He turned to Devora and said, "And if there's time will you play *dreidel* with me tonight? For money?"

"For money," his sister reluctantly agreed.

Later that night, after Havdala, Yossi and his guests set up all the menoras on a small table so that they could be seen through the front window. Devora had brought her own menora with her. It was the one her uncle had given her; she had been using it since she was five. As she held the *shammas* to the candle she tried to concentrate on what she was feeling so that she could write the essay for Morah Chana. But her mind wouldn't focus—all she could think of was another menora in an abandoned building in the woods.

Chaim, however, was moping. He thought about his missing menora and that this year he wouldn't be able to light it.

Soon all the menoras were lit. Candles glowed brightly in the window and filled the room with a warm light. Yossi began singing *Maoz Tzur*. Rebbe Doresh and Chaim joined in with a lusty harmony. After they'd sung a few more traditional Chanukah songs Devora looked over at her brother and suggested with a smile, "Chaim, why don't you sing your solo for us?" Chaim was more than happy to comply with that request. When the applause had waned, everyone put on his or her coat and got ready to leave.

Just before leaving the house, Devora remembered she'd left her new detective set behind. She ran upstairs and pulled the survival kit from her suitcase. She hoped she would have the opportunity to use it in a real detective case.

The first stop was Mina's house. Yossi was very nervous. His hand shook as he rang the bell. But the house was dark, and no one came to answer the door.

"Well, I guess that's that," he said, shrugging his shoulders in despair.

"Come, let's head over to the shul. Maybe we can still find the *geniza,*" said Yossi.

They drove to the edge of the woods and Yossi led the way with his lantern. Inside the shul he put the lantern on the *bima.*

The light from the lantern cast mysterious shadows around the room. Mrs. Doresh shook her head and shuddered. "The faster we get out of here the better," she told Rebbe Doresh. He smiled and walked over to the wall on the right side and flicked on a switch.

The room lit up. "I thought Mr. Solomon couldn't be against electricity . . . the Shul may have a menora but it also has recessed lighting."

Devora put her hands against the Bima and tried to push it. "This thing won't budge. Let's go inside the other room and try moving the menora, maybe the *geniza's* hidden under the floor boards.

They all marched into the other section. The menora loomed before them like a cactus in the desert. Mrs. Doresh tried to straighten out the twisted branches but it was useless. Although it was easy to swing the branches back into shape, it was just as easy for them to swing themselves back out of shape. "This place is creepy," conceded Chaim after a few minutes. "Listen to it . . . The whole Shul sounds like it needs an oil job."

Mrs. Doresh bent down and picked up a sheet of paper she found on the floor. "What's this? I think it's the Bnei Shem announcement that you brought us from the newspaper office." She showed the flyer to Devora. "I guess Mina is preparing for the takeover."

Rebbe Doresh shook his head and frowned. "To think that this Shul will now be used by Apikorsim who wish to turn away our own people. I wish there would be a way to stop them."

"There is nothing we can do," Chaim answered glumly.

"Don't give up so easily," said Devora. "In the time of the Greeks, the Jews never gave up, no matter how bad things got. Hashem is always with us—even now. Maybe tomorrow night we can come back and light the menora. It's true that it may be the last time this Shul will have its menora lit for a Jewish holiday . . . but we have to try our best. This Shul must not be destroyed. We owe it to the founders of the shul to try and re-dedicate it, just like the Jews rededicated the Holy Temple at Chanukah time."

Mrs. Doresh wiped away a tear. "What a splendid idea . . . but first, let's clean up the mess." She sniffed the air in the room. It seemed old and musty. Chaim saw his mother's look. He recognized her 'clean-up-

mood' but he too suddenly got caught up in the excitement of Devora's words.

"I'll clean the window and open it," he offered.

"I'll dust the Menora and the pews," said Mrs.
Doresh.

"I have rags in the trunk of my car," offered Yossi,
"but if you wish, I can drive home and bring a broom."

"Look what I found," Chaim announced as he held
up something in his hand. It was a gold ring. The top of
the ring had a menora design.

Yossi took it from him and held it carefully. "It's
Mina's" he explained. "Her father had this thing about
Chanukah. It's hard to explain. I never heard of anything like it before. He really loved the holiday. He was
married on Chanukah, both his daughters were born on
Chanukah . . . he started his first successful business ven-
ture on Chanukah. He gave this ring to Mina on her
birthday. He gave one to her sister also . . ." His voice
broke while he was talking . . . "I don't understand
what's happened . . . I don't understand why any of this
is happening now . . ."

Mrs. Doresh interrupted everyone's thoughts. "I
don't want to spend the whole night here . . . so if
we're going to clean up let's do it now . . . and I'm
going to start with the menora!"

"I'll go into the other room and dust the bima,"

offered Devora. "We'll make the whole shul look beautiful in no time."

Devora began straightening some of the chairs. She heard Yossi's car drive away, and heard the sound of her father's voice. He did not want to leave the family alone in this strange place. Rebbe Doresh peeked into the room where Devora was moving a bench and tossed a rag at her. "Here, just do a little dusting . . . we don't want to stay here too long . . ." and then he turned around and left Devora alone. As she began to dust, she sat down on the steps leading up to the bima and leaned back against it. In the other room, her father and her brother had begun to sing a Chanukah song. Devora closed her eyes and listened.

Suddenly the bima began to move, and before she had a chance to realize what had happened the floor gave way beneath her and she fell for what seemed an eternity. When she finally hit the ground she looked around her, dazed. The opening she had fallen through had closed and she found herself in total darkness. Reaching into her pocket for the survival kit, she found the miniature flashlight and switched it on. When she saw where she was she gasped. She was in a tunnel directly underneath the bima.

As she tried to get up she felt a sharp pain in her left foot and reached out to grab something to help her

stand up. Shining her flashlight around the room, she was surprised to see a twisted wooden menora cemented down on the floor in the tunnel. But the pain in her foot distracted her again. I hope it's not broken, she thought, and then she remembered she had plans to go skating with Shaindy on Tuesday.

She finally got to her feet, and beamed her flashlight at the ceiling. The trap door had closed so completely that she was no longer sure of her location. She screamed as loudly and as unprofessionally as she could: "Abba! Mommy! Abba!" It was to no avail. A chill ran through her body as she realized her father and mother might not have even noticed her disappearance.

There must be a way out of here, Devora reasoned with herself. This tunnel was probably like the tunnel in the Touro synagogue her teacher had described. One of the oldest shuls in the country, the building was constructed with a tunnel underneath the *bima* so that the congregants could escape in case of a surprise attack by the Indians. And there was another tunnel she had learned about in school—if only she could remember where it was, it might give her a clue as to how to escape. Oh, yes, the cave of Zedekiah. When Jerusalem had fallen to Nebuchadnezzer, King Zedekiah made a tunnel all the way to Jericho by traveling through a cave under his castle. If so, and if the tunnel she was in was anything like the other two—why then, there must be a way out! If she would only walk far enough she would have to find it.

She began walking cautiously in what she hoped was the opposite direction of the *bima*. It was obvious from the layers of dust and cobwebs which were all around that the tunnel hadn't been used in years. Her foot was really hurting now, and her mouth was parched and full of dust. She felt really sick.

As the light of her flashlight danced along the walls of the cave, Devora aimed it at the wooden menora she had seen. It, too, had twisted branches, just like the one upstairs. She lifted one drooping branch and heard a creak, like the sound of a door opening. She moved her flashlight along the floor and walls and saw an open cabinet. Holding the flashlight straight, Devora focused on some objects to her left. She saw a large glass bookcase and five beautiful *Sefer Torahs* dressed in the silver splendor, reflecting back at her. Though tarnished with age, their Ataros still gleamed and sparkled. Next to this bookcase stood yet another . . . a credenza of Seforim. . . . The *geniza!* She had found the *geniza!*

Her nerves were tingling with excitement. She was afraid to touch the yellowing pages. For the moment an eerie feeling of doom enveloped the tunnel. She quietly whispered the *Shema* to herself and then took a deep breath. She must find the opening and show the world the treasures in this tunnel.

After hobbling through the tunnel for what seemed like miles, Devora found herself in front of a stone wall. The tunnel did not go further. She moved her hands carefully around the wall . . . perhaps there was an opening. She began to shiver and felt faint. Her eyes followed a spider as it crept along the wall.

Suddenly she heard a sound . . . she didn't know from where and she stepped back quickly. She almost tripped over yet another twisted menora that was cemented to the ground. As she picked up a drooping branch, she heard a creaking sound and looked to the wall and gasped. A line began to cut through the wall like a knife cutting through a piece of meat. It took her a few seconds to realize that a door was opening in front of her. She stood up quickly and limped towards the opening. But first she took a loose rock and stuck it by the door to block it from closing all the way. She thought for a minute about what had just happened. The menora's branch was a lever to open a trap door! So that's what must have happened upstairs! And that's how she had uncovered the *geniza!*

Devora found herself in a walk-in closet. Two rows of ladies clothes flanked either side of the entrance. In front of her was a closed door. She breathed a sigh of relief and moved forward to open the door. As she reached for it she hesitated for a moment. Had she heard voices from the other side? Devora put her ear to the

door and listened intently. Yes, someone was inside . . .
in fact she heard two distinctly different voices. She
looked through the peephole and saw a woman tied to a
chair facing the closet door. The other speaker was
standing sideways near the chair. She seemed hesitant
and unsure of herself. Devora was getting dizzy staring
through the peephole, so she sat down on the floor and
pressed her ear against the door.

"Please Ora, let me go. I wouldn't harm you for
anything in the world. You're my sister . . ."

Ora shifted uncomfortably. "Why should I believe
you? You have already betrayed me once, Mina."

"Ora, I only want to do what's best for both of us.
Father knew what he was doing when he left this
property to me. He didn't want his precious synagogue
to fall into the hands of idol-worshippers! Yossi and I
wanted to reopen the shul and make it into a spiritual
center for Peabody's Jews, just as it was in the days of
our great-great grandfather," said Mina.

"But Shem wants to do the same thing. He also
wants to make the synagogue into a spiritual center—
for anyone who wants to join," said Ora in a shaking
voice. "Even you agreed with the idea, and then you
backed out on the agreement. I don't think you can be
trusted, Mina."

"Do you know the whole story, or does Shem just
tell you what he wants you to hear? Did he tell you

under what circumstances I agreed to turn the shul over to you as part of your inheritance?" said Mina. "He threatened to harm you, my sister, if I didn't agree. So I went to City Hall and drew up some phoney documents to appease Shem. When Shem found out what I had done, he had you come over to my house to entice me to come to the shul where we could 'talk.' That's when your friend Shem decided to tie me up in this room, to keep me out of the way."

"But Shem told me that I was to inherit this building—and I should contact you once and for all and claim my property. He said that you were lying when you told me Abba left everything to you."

"Think a minute, Ora, about who is lying and who is telling the truth. Listen to me, Ora . . . we are sisters. Both of us were raised as religious Jews. How could you throw everything away for a liar, for a group who doesn't believe in Hashem . . . or in anything that we know of as truth? What good did Shem ever do for you . . . all these years you've been living a nightmare."

"I'm afraid, I'm afraid!" answered Ora, rubbing her fingers nervously, fighting back tears.

"It is Chanukah tonight," said Mina, still tied to the chair. "It is a holiday our father always cherished. Dare we turn away from something he loved?"

Devora shifted her position as she looked through the peephole again. She saw the faces clearly . . . the one tied to the chair had long blonde hair tied in a ponytail behind her head . . . the other one had her blonde hair cropped short and close to the face. They looked very much alike.

"Please, let's go back to my house and light the Chanukah menora. Do it for our father, if not for me."

"You know something? I was walking in the woods the other day and found a battered, brass menora by a tree. I picked it up and took it home, for sentimental reasons I guess. I felt that someone was trying to tell me something, to remind me about Chanukah. It always was my favorite holiday," sobbed Ora as she burst into tears.

Ora bent down next to her sister and tried to untie the ropes, but they wouldn't loosen. She searched through the dresser drawers and found a nail file and some matches. This time she was successful. With her wrists free, the long-haired woman began rubbing her hands to regain circulation. She stood up and took her sister by the hand. "Let's go before Shem comes back," said Mina gently.

Just then a door opened and a strange-looking man appeared. Devora heard a raspy male voice and stood up. "I told you to guard her, not to set her free. So you are thinking of joining your family again? Returning to Judaism?" he said mockingly. "We'll have to retrain you," he began to taunt, "but first, I think it's time we got rid of your sister."

Devora realized that something terrible was about to happen. She began to open the closet door slowly. She pushed her hands forward and thrust the figure in dark clothing towards the dresser. Stunned by this movement behind him, he fell down in a daze. "Hurry," she called to the two standing in shock near the menora. "Hurry . . . follow me," she called again.

Mina began moving towards her, while her sister Ora hesitated. Devora grabbed Ora by the arm, turned and stepped back into the closet. She slipped her fingers between the opening of the tunnel door, pushed it open and kicked away the stone. The two sisters followed her into the tunnel.

"I think we can lock this door from here so he can't get out," said Devora.

"You're right," said Mina, "but I hear him trying to break down the closet door that enters into the tunnel. I think we'd better get moving fast."

They heard a crashing sound . . . and the clutter of footsteps behind them.

"Hurry, hurry!" Devora suddenly tripped and fell. "Oh no," she lamented. "My ankle, I don't think I can walk anymore."

"We'll help you," said Mina. "We will support you . . ."

The two girls grabbed her, each by an elbow, and helped her move along the tunnel as quickly as they possibly could.

Finally they came to the end and the sisters stood bewildered. They heard Shem's footsteps coming closer and they didn't know what to do.

"I know," said Devora as she reached towards the menora cemented down into the floor. "*Boruch Hashem,* I know," she said with a smile. She reached for the wooden menora that she had seen when she had first fallen through the *bima* and twisted its branch back into place.

"Look," shouted Ora, "a trap door above us . . ."

The wood slid slowly away and they were soon staring at the shul's high ceiling. It looked beautiful . . . but the footsteps from the other end of the tunnel were approaching even closer.

The sisters were panic-stricken. "It's Shem. He's coming back for us!"

"How will we ever get up there?" asked Ora.

Devora began screaming. "Abba! Mommy! Help! Help!" The two girls joined in: "Help! Help!"

"Abba! Mommy! Yossi! Abba! Help!"

Finally Rebbe Doresh's face appeared in the opening above them.

"Hurry!" shouted Mina. "Get us out of here!"

Suddenly a policeman appeared. He jumped down into the tunnel and drew his gun.

Rebbe Doresh and Yossi lowered a ladder, and the girls climbed out.

When Devora next opened her eyes she found herself in bed. She looked around slowly trying to figure out how she had gotten there. It was no use . . . she couldn't remember a thing and trying to figure it out made her head throb. She was about to go back to sleep when she noticed the clock said ten minutes of two. It had to be daytime, because sunlight was streaming in the open window. Suddenly she felt a sharp pain in her leg. Now she was beginning to remember everything! She hesitantly pulled her covers off and looked at her leg. The last time she had looked it was streaming blood. Now there was a big bandage around it. Devora forced herself to get out of bed and limped over to her clothes. After she finished dressing herself she limped down to the living room and found her mother sitting in a big antique chair, reading a magazine.

"Mom?" Devora said quietly.

Mrs. Doresh turned around. Judging from the bags under her eyes, she hadn't slept all night.

"Good morning, young lady. Did you have a good sleep?"

Devora nodded and looked hesitantly at her mother.

"When did my leg get bandaged? And by whom?"

Mrs. Doresh smiled. "You really don't remember? Well, it's probably only natural. You were quite weak and had lost a great deal of blood from that wound. We took you to the hospital and in the emergency room they gave you six stitches. They also gave you a pain-killer—that's what put you to sleep."

Devora shook her head in amazement. She didn't remember a thing about what her mother was telling her. The last thing she remembered was seeing her father walking towards her.

At that moment the front door swung open. In walked Yossi, Mina, Chaim and Rebbe Doresh. As soon as they saw Devora up and awake, they crowded round her asking excited questions.

Leaving her daughter to field the questions by herself, Mrs. Doresh got up and went to the kitchen. Soon the aroma of frying *latkes* filled the air. Chaim escorted his sister over to the table and pulled out her chair. Soon everyone had his share of *latkes* and the table was buzzing with happy conversation.

Devora, however, kept silent. Things were moving too fast for her. She looked over at Yossi and Mina. They looked very happy now. There were so many questions she wanted to ask, but was hesitant about bringing them up. Where was Ora? What happened to Shem? What happened to the broken engagement?

Suddenly Devora gave a small gasp. She had noticed in the tunnel that Mina's hair was nearly down to her waist, and now that it had been washed and combed Devora could see how lovely it really was. But Yossi had told them that when he walked into the Solomon house on the day Mina broke the engagement, the first thing he had noticed was that Mina had cut her hair. She turned to Yossi, "I thought you said that Mina had cut her hair short."

Yossi blushed and smiled. "When I went to Mina's house it was her sister Ora I had spoken to. I was so upset that I didn't realize it wasn't Mina. They do look alike, you know. It was Ora who broke the engagement. Should I say, it was Ora who *didn't* break the engagement, because it wasn't hers to break. Thanks to you, Devora, we are back together. Furthermore, Devora, we have decided to 'rededicate' the shul, just like the Hasmoneans rededicated the *Bais HaMikdash* more than 2,000 years ago. Mina and I wanted to give you a chance to recover, and to clean up the place. So we are going to be lighting our menoras, God willing, tomorrow night at the old Solomon shul. You and your family will be the guests of honor."

Devora was so excited—she wanted to jump up and down for joy, but she couldn't because of her bandaged foot. "Abba, can we really stay another day and witness this exciting event?"

"Of course," said Rebbe Doresh. "We have a lot to celebrate—the reopening of the shul, its redemption from evildoers, Yossi and Mina's unbroken engagement, and Mina and Ora's birthdays. We will also give special thanks to Hashem that Ora has agreed to stay with Mina for a while—and away from Shem who is now in jail. It is going to be difficult, but Ora has agreed to work with Yossi's friend Mayer, a rabbi who has had success with Jewish kids who have been mixed up with cults and missionaries."

Just then the door opened and Ora walked in. She was smiling as Mina arose and welcomed her with a hug. Devora looked at the two sisters. They really did look very much alike even though one had longer hair than the other. Ora took Devora's hand and squeezed it gently. "I really must thank you so much for everything. When I left home, I was angry at everyone . . . most of all, Hashem. I loved my mother dearly and couldn't understand why Hashem found it necessary to take her from us. I guess I still don't know the answer to that question, but I do know, that He really didn't leave me alone. My father and my sister still loved me very much. I know my father looked for me . . . once I was almost caught by one of his detectives but with Shem's help I always eluded them. Then one day, just a couple of weeks ago, Shem told me that I was to inherit this house, the shul and all the land around it. He wanted me to claim my inheritance and donate it to the commune. I wanted to do anything Shem asked of me but when we arrived here we learned that my father had left everything to my sister . . . I was angry all over again so it was easy for Shem to convince me to take Mina's place. He promised me that no harm would come to her."

"Even when he tied your sister up?"

"It did bother me, but I trusted Shem. Well, that first night of Chanukah, Mina and I had a long talk and I realized that the only reason I was not mentioned in the will was that my father was afraid that I would do exactly what I had begun to do . . . but he had made Mina promise that should I ever return and still follow the faith of our father, she was to divide the inheritance evenly."

"What actually happened to Shem?" asked Devora.

"The police have him on kidnapping charges," said Yossi. "And I think they have a few more charges against him as well. He'll be locked away for some time."

"He really is an evil man," said Ora. "I guess I never wanted to believe it."

"Then your father was right," said Devora. "Chanukah was truly a happy holiday for the Solomons . . ."

"But not for me," said Chaim, "because I lost my menora."

Devora leaned over and whispered something to Ora. The girl smiled and walked out.

Meanwhile, Yossi came in holding a parchment. "This *geniza* is fantastic," he said. "Look, this is a condolence letter from General Ulysses S. Grant, dated 1864. It's a condolence letter written to Rabbi Solomon about his son who was killed fighting under Grant's command. This letter is worth a fortune!" He was very excited. "Did you see the *Sifre Torah* and the *Siddurim?*" Yossi was jubilant. His plans of reopening the Shul would come to fruition after all. With the money they would get from Grant's letter and the *geniza*, they would be able to create a real haven for young Jews. Everyone seemed excited for him.

"Wait a minute," said Chaim, "I still don't understand how you opened the trap door!"

"I didn't," explained Devora. "Mother did. You see, this is really a house of menoras . . . even the tunnel had two! But the strangest part was that all the menoras were twisted. I knew there had to be a reason. I discovered that by twisting a branch back into shape we inadvertently opened a trap door somewhere. I assume the builders of the Shul had their reason for placing the menora in one room and the entrance to the tunnel under the *bima*, in the other room. Even in the tunnel, the menora is the key to open the door. As mother was

dusting the menora, I was leaning against the *bima* . . .
you didn't see me fall . . . but I sure did!"

"Then the twisted menora was the clue to finding
the *geniza* after all!"

"Definitely," she nodded, and then her eyes lit up as
Ora came back into the room. She was holding a brass
menora. Chaim jumped up and laughed. "Where did
you find it?"

"I think your menora found me . . ." she explained.

Later that evening Devora went lazily to bed. Her
mother looked at her and smiled before her eyes closed
for the night. "I guess, Mr. Solomon really loved this
holiday very much," said Devora. "So much so that he
even named his daughters in honor of the symbol of the
festivities . . . Mina and Ora.

As Mrs. Doresh mused over Devora's discovery,
Devora thought of how moved she was by the sisters'
story. Suddenly she realized she had an answer for
Morah Chana's assignment. The light of the Chanukah
menora reminded her of Hashem and how He is always
close even when we seem to be far away. Devora
would never have found Mina were it not for the sign
of the twisted menora. And it was Chaim's Chanukah
menora that rekindled Ora's feelings for her family and
her people. Finally, it was Chanukah which brought
the two sisters back together again. Devora remem-

bered the saying in the Talmud that Morah Chana had taught them: "The *mitzvah* is the lamp and the Torah is the light." Now she understood what it meant.

As she lay in bed, Devora thought of Chaim and his menora . . . she took a deep breath and closed her eyes and said the *Shema,* and as she moved off into dreamland her last thoughts were . . . Shema Yisrael . . . Hear O Israel . . . the Menora of Israel . . . the light of Israel shall glow forever.

The Russian Connection

The sound of laughter filled the house. Music was blasting from the record player, and everyone in the family was either clapping or humming or tapping his feet to the Chanukah songs. The delicious aroma of homemade potato latkes wafted in from the kitchen as Devora spun the *dreidle*. She and her little brother Chaim were teaching the traditional Chanukah game to Boris Penkovsky. The three of them sat at the dining room table and watched intently as the small top wobbled and finally came to rest on one of its four sides, with one Hebrew letter showing.

"Shin—Put in!" shouted Chaim. "Put another penny in, Devora. Oboyoboy . . . now I'm gonna win the whole pot!" He picked up the *dreidle* and spun it with a flourish. "Come onnn . . . *Gimmel!* come onnnn . . . *Gimmel!* It's stopping—its stopping —it's—"

"Shin," said Devora with a smile. "Put in another penny, hotshot." She passed the *dreidle* to Boris. "Remember which is which?"

"I think so . . . let me see. If it comes up 'Shin,' you put in, and with 'Gimmel' you get the whole pot. 'Hay,' you take half and 'Nun' means you do nothing."

Boris was a Russian immigrant who had been in America only six months. Shortly after his arrival he had met the Doresh family, and they had all been good friends ever since. He spun the dreidle and continued talking. "You know, it's very strange. In Russia I used to dream of the day when I'd be able to hear Jewish singing and play Jewish games right out in the open. But somehow this game doesn't seem very Jewish. Except for the Hebrew letters on the dreidle."

Devora explained. "Back in the days when Israel was ruled by the Hellenized Syrians, the Jews were not allowed to study Torah. I guess it was something like what is happening in Russia today. The people used to gather together in secret and post spies all around the hiding places. When someone was coming, the spies would signal them, and everyone pretended to be playing dreidle. So since Chanukah is all about the miracles that happened in those days, dreidle became a Chanukah game."

"We could have used some dreidles back in Moscow," laughed Boris. "We—" But he was interrupted by a sudden squeal from Chaim.

"Gimmel! You got Gimmel! You win it all!"

The candles in the Chanukah menora were burning low. Everyone had sung 'Haneiros Hallalu' and 'Maoz Tzur,' and Rebbe Doresh had told some wonderful stories of the days of the Maccabbees and the Hasmonaim. Mrs. Doresh was the first to get up from the couch.

"Latkes, anyone?"

The family and their Russian guest all sat around the dining room table enjoying the holiday meal, especially the hot potato pancakes with applesauce. Boris took his third helping and then passed the tray to Devora. "Would you like some more?"

"*Spaceba!*"

"Why, Devora—I didn't know you speak Russian!"

"Only a few words, Boris." She smiled shyly. "There are some Russian girls in my school, and I've been giving them private lessons to help them catch up with their English. So they teach me Russian in return."

"Well, then maybe we could do the same. I'll help you with your Russian and you can teach me Yiddish."

"You've got yourself a deal! And it shouldn't be too hard for you, since you already know Hebrew—not to mention about a zillion other languages."

Boris laughed. "Only six or seven. I was a professor of Romance Languages at the University. My father taught me Hebrew; he specialized in the Semitic Languages."

"Didn't that have something to do with the way you escaped from Russia?"

"Yes, it did," said Boris, as he stared down at the latke on his plate. There was a long pause. Boris sighed

and thought to himself for a moment about the events
of the past year of his life. "So did my father's death.
You see, about a year ago some ancient Semitic writings
were discovered in Egypt and then brought to Italy.
My father wanted very much to see the scrolls, and so
did his associate, my friend Nikolai Ratsky. The Com-
missariat didn't want to let them go at first, especially
since my father was Jewish. They suspected that he
wanted to leave Russia. But with my father they had
nothing to worry about. He loved his country and
would never have left. Anyway, the day the visa finally
came through was the day he died. My mother told me
to go in my father's place, and run away. She said I
would never be able to advance myself in Russia, and
she knew how much I hated the government there.
Nikolai encouraged me too. He also wanted to get out
of Russia, although he's not Jewish. So I disguised
myself as an older man and Nikolai and I went to Italy.
From there we escaped together to this country."

"Whatever happened to Nikolai?" asked Rebbe
Doresh.

"He's here in New York. In fact I'm going to be seeing him later tonight. He has some kind of job at a
hospital in Manhattan. Just yesterday he called me and
suggested we get together and talk over old times. I've
only spoken to him a couple of times since we arrived.
Nikolai and I used to be like brothers. We even look

alike. When he began to study Semitics people were always taking him for my father's son. Ah, the old times . . . But listen to me! Here I am a young man and blabbering about the old times!" He shrugged his shoulders, smiled, and polished off the rest of his meal.

After they cleaned off the table Boris excused himself. "I don't want to seem like an ungrateful guest, but I really must go now. Thank you all for a wonderful time—and for the latkes!"

Chaim raced over to the hall closet. "I'll get your coat!"

A little later Chaim and Devora played another round of dreidle, and this time Chaim won handily. "Somehow," said Devora, "I think you're cheating, but I can't for the life of me figure out how."

"It's just my magic fingers," snickered Chaim. He reached deep into both pants pockets and pulled out two handfuls of assorted dreidles. "Here, choose any one you want. Cheating? Hah! I'll beat you with any dreidle you choose. And if these aren't enough for you, I've got some big ones back in my room."

Just then the doorbell rang, and they heard their mother's expression of surprise when she opened the door. After a few minutes Devora's father called her into the living room. Standing by the mantelpiece was none other than Sergeant O'Malley. He looked tired, and he was speaking to Rabbi and Mrs. Doresh.

"I'm sorry to have interrupted you on your holiday, but I have no one else to turn to at the moment. We know that Lex got the information out of Russia, and we know where it is supposed to be hidden, but without your help we'll never find it."

"What are you talking about?" asked Devora. "Who's Lex?"

"Alexander Yalov." The sergeant turned to Devora and smiled. "Hi, kiddo. I'm sorry. Let me fill you in. Lex was an American newspaper reporter working in Russia, but he was also acting as an American agent."

"Was?"

"He's here now. A few days ago he managed to obtain a very important list of Russian spies working in the United States, and planned to smuggle it out of the country himself. Well, when Lex stepped off the plane here in New York, he was shot by a mysterious attacker in the airport lobby. He's in the hospital now, completely paralyzed on one side and unable to speak. So he can't tell us where the list is hidden."

Devora interrupted him. "But I thought I heard you saying you know where it's supposed to be."

"The list was photographed on microfilm—no larger than a tiny dot. All we know is that the dot is hidden somewhere in the pages of some books that Lex brought back among his personal belongings . . .

Hebrew books. And that's where your father comes in."

Rebbe Doresh looked up in surprise. "You mean you want me to examine his books?"

"Exactly. Somewhere in the middle of all those dots and lines and squiggles is our microdot. One of the CIA agents on the case is an old buddy of mine from the Police Academy, and he remembered my telling him about Devora's investigative skills." Devora smiled sheepishly at the sergeant. So he called me up, figuring that as a Rabbi you would be able to decipher a dot where it doesn't belong in all that writing. I came right over after speaking with him."

"Of course, I'd be more than happy to help you if I possibly can," said Rebbe Doresh. "Where are the books now?"

"All of Lex's things were brought with him to the hospital. If you don't mind I'd like you to go over there with me now. Devora is welcome to come along if she wants to."

Rebbe Doresh looked at his daughter. "What do you say, do you think you'd mind working together with your father on a case?"

Devora grinned. "What kind of a question is that?"

It was a long ride into Manhattan and uptown to Mount Sinai Hospital. When Sergeant O'Malley and the Doreshes arrived on the third floor where Lex

Yalov was staying, the hospital corridor was swarming with uniformed and plainclothes police. The sergeant rushed over to one of them and asked what was going on.

"There was an attempted murder. Someone got into Yalov's room and was about to smother him with a pillow when one of the nurses walked in. He ran before he could do anything, but he got away. We have a pretty good description, and we put out an APB. Oh, yeah—there was also a piece of evidence he seems to have left behind—a monogrammed handkerchief."

"Where's Wilcox?"

"Down the hall in Yalov's room."

"Thanks," said Sergeant O'Malley. He gestured to the Doreshes. "Let's go."

As they were walking down the long hallway, Rebbe Doresh asked quietly, "What's an APB?" Devora answered him before the Sergeant had a chance to speak.

"An All Points Bulletin. Every policeman in the city will have his description."

Tom Wilcox of the CIA greeted his old friend warmly. "Well, O'Malley, it's about time you got here. It's not like you to miss all the action. Things have been pretty hot up here for the last half hour."

"So I've been told, Tom, so I've been told. Let's be thankful they weren't any hotter. How's Lex?"

"The guy actually never laid a hand on him. His condition is stable; he's conscious, but he still can't talk. The doctors have no idea when—or if—he will regain control of his muscles. Meanwhile, as you can see, we've tightened up the security. But you haven't introduced me to your friends."

The sergeant made the introductions, and Wilcox beamed as he shook the Rabbi's hand. "I feel as if I already know you. Your friend has spoken very highly of you both."

In an adjoining room were all of Lex Yalov's belongings, and Inspector Wilcox wasted no time in explaining to Rebbe Doresh exactly what they were looking for. "We've gone through the cloth bindings on all the books, and found nothing. But we're practically certain that it's in one of the books—Lex has used this method several times before. He simply places the dot among the Hebrew letters. But the other times he was able to tell us where it was."

Spread out on a small table were all of Lex Yalov's religious articles, and a half-dozen Hebrew books. There was a velvet *tallis* bag, a silver chain with a small *mezuzah* charm attached to it, a thin bracelet designed to look like two tablets with the Ten Commandments engraved on them, and a small wooden dreidle. Devora and her father began looking through the books. "This could take forever," she said to herself. They sat there long into the night, turning page after page after page, until Devora was so tired the letters on the pages were swimming in front of her eyes.

Devora decided to leave the rest of the books to her father; she couldn't even see straight any more. She looked at the bracelet, the *tallis* bag, and the other items on the table, but she couldn't see anything on them that looked like a microdot, either. Absent-mindedly, she picked up the dreidel and gave it a spin. "Shin again," she muttered to herself. "That's just my kind of luck. Even when I play by myself I get stuck with Shin!" There was something unusual about the Shin, she sensed, but she was too tired to figure it out.

Suddenly there was a loud commotion in the other room, and a minute later Sergeant O'Malley opened the door and said excitedly, "We've got him! A man who fit the description was found hanging around in the lobby of the hospital, and the nurse just made a positive identification. He must have been waiting for a chance to try and finish the job!"

Devora heard a loud voice from the hallway protesting, "I am telling you, this is a terrible mistake. I know nothing about this! I have never seen this man in my life!" There was something familiar about the voice, but Devora was so tired she couldn't place it. But when she went out to have a look in the corridor, she couldn't believe her eyes.

"Boris! What are you—"

"Devora!" shouted Boris. "What are *you* doing here?"

And Rebbe Doresh came out a second later and was equally shocked. "Boris Penkovsky! What in the world are you doing here?" Sergeant O'Malley and Inspector Wilcox looked at each other in utter confusion and then turned back to the Doreshes and their suspect. "You mean you people know each other?"

"Of course we know each other," answered Rebbe Doresh. "We were together just this afternoon. But Boris, I don't understand. How did you get mixed up in all this?"

"Mixed up in all *what*, Rabbi? I have no idea what is happening here. I was waiting downstairs in the lobby to meet my friend Nikolai Ratsky, as I told you earlier. When he did not come, I went to the desk to ask a nurse if he could be paged or something. But as soon as I began to speak she began to act very strangely, and before I knew it these police officers had me handcuffed and up here for questioning. And I have not understood one of their questions yet. There has been a terrible mistake. Please, Rabbi, Devora, tell them who I am!"

The police took statements from everyone, and Sergeant O'Malley was very sorry that the Doresh's friend was implicated in the attempted murder, but there was too much evidence against him to let him go. One of the doctors in the Hospital had confirmed the nurse's identification of Boris as the man who was seen running from the room. And the clincher was the handkerchief they had found next to Yalov's bed. It was monogrammed with the initial 'P'—for Penkovsky.

"Sounds like circumstantial evidence to me," said Rebbe Doresh.

"Circumstantial or not," said the Sergeant, "I'm afraid we're going to have to hold your friend. At this point he's all we've got."

On the way home in Sergeant O'Malley's car, Rebbe Doresh apologized for not being able to find the microdot. "But I'll try again if you would like me to," he said.

"Me too," said Devora sadly. She was very upset to have seen her friend Boris being taken off to prison. She didn't want to leave, but her father had insisted. It was very late, he had said, and tomorrow was a school day. Somewhere in the middle of the Brooklyn Battery Tunnel Devora drifted off to sleep.

The next day in school Devora could hardly pay attention. She kept thinking about Boris Penkovsky sitting in a jail cell, and about the missing microdot. She was sure that Boris had to be innocent, but how could they prove it? All the evidence seemed to . . .

"Some of us don't seem to be listening, Devora." It was Morah Hartman, the Hebrew teacher. "Are we off on another mystery this morning?"

"Uh, yes, I guess so. I'm sorry, Morah. I didn't get much sleep last night. I'll try to be more alert."

"An excellent idea, Devora. Now, if we can get back to the B'nei Efraim. . . ?"

They were studying the portion of *Shoftim,* the Book of Judges, about the Bnei Efraim and Gilead. The Bnei Efraim were idol-worshippers who tried to hide their identity during the war with the Gileadites. But they were found out because they could not pronounce the word 'shibboleth'; they could only say 'sibboleth.' They mistook the letter 'Shin' for a 'Sin.'

When the school bell rang, Devora picked up her books and began walking slowly to the study hall. She had a free period coming up and had arranged to give an English lesson to Natasha Rostov, one of the Russian girls at school. All during the next half-hour she couldn't stop thinking about the Bnei Efraim. Then Natasha opened up her Russian grammar book and reviewed the Russian alphabet with Devora . . . and it was then that Devora had the idea.

Sergeant O'Malley pulled up in the blue and white police car to the front of the Yocheved High School, and Devora got in. "Okay, so what's all this about?" he asked her. "This better be a good one. You wouldn't believe what kind of a day this has been down at the station house."

"I'll explain everything when we get to the hospital. Will Inspector Wilcox be there?"

"Yes, he will. I called him right after I spoke to you on the phone. He was planning to look in on Lex anyway."

"Fine."

Once up on the third floor of Mount Sinai Hospital, Devora marched straight into the room with Lex Yalov's belongings. She went over to the table, pushed the books aside, and picked up the dreidle. "Inspector," she said, "I think I have found your microdot, but it's only a wild guess."

"Where?"

Devora handed him the dreidle. "Do you see this little dot? Well, it doesn't belong there. A dreidle is supposed to have a 'Shin,' and a Shin has a dot on the upper *right*-hand corner. This letter, however, is a 'Sin.' The dot is on the left."

Wilcox and O'Malley examined the dreidle. "You know, Tom," said the sergeant, "I think she's right. Look here—it seems like this dot is pasted on with some sort of adhesive. Let's get this down to the lab right away."

"Uh, Sergeant," said Devora, "there's something else. You have arrested the wrong man."

"You said that yesterday, Devora, but the evidence—"

"Is that handkerchief still here?"

"No, of course not. We brought it back to the station last night. The district attorney will be looking it over just about now."

"Well, you'd better call him right away. I think you'll find that the handkerchief was manufactured in Russia."

Wilcox interrupted her. "Certainly it was. We were able to determine that this morning. But what's your point? It still has Penkovsky's initial."

"No, inspector, it doesn't. I realized today that the Russian letter 'P' is pronounced like our 'R' in English. That handkerchief could not have belonged to Boris. And I bet you'll find that Nikolai Ratsky is your man."

"Nikolai who?"

"Ratsky. You see, Boris told us yesterday that he had a friend who escaped Russia together with him, and that he worked in the hospital. That's what Boris was doing there. He was supposed to meet Nikolai here last night, but Nikolai was obviously too busy to show up. In Russian, the name Ratsky begins with a letter that looks like 'P.'* Check with the hospital for Ratsky's address, and there you find your Russian assassin."

*АБВГДЕЕЖЗИЙКЛМНОПРСТУФХЦЧШШЩЪЫЬЭЮЯ
абвгдеёжзийклмнопрстуфхцчшшщъыьэюя

"Would-be assassin," corrected Sergeant O'Malley. "Devora, I do believe you've done it again."

The next evening, Sergeant O'Malley, Inspector Wilcox, and Boris Penkovsky were sitting in the Doresh living room drinking tea and eating Mrs. Doresh's homemade honey cake. Boris was speaking.

"So you see, as I was telling Devora the other day, Nikolai and I were always mistaken for brothers ever since we were children. That was why the nurse was so sure that he was me—I mean, that I was him. But I still cannot believe that Nikolai is a Communist spy."

"Well, it's true, he is," said Wilcox. "Our men at the microfilm lab confirmed today that his name was right up there at the top of the list. And we have him safely in our custody now. He wasn't home when we checked out the address last night, but we posted a guard at the hospital and he was captured this morning coming out of the third floor elevator. Seems he was trying to get back into Lex's room."

Boris shook his head sadly. "And to think that I trusted Nikolai all these years. And to think that they used my father as part of the plot . . ." He fell silent for a moment and then let out a deep sigh. "It certainly is reassuring to know that there are still people like Devora and her family left in the world."

Inspector Wilcox finished off his cup of tea and smiled at Boris. "Looks like we all have Devora to thank for this one."

"Don't thank me," Devora laughed, "thank the Gileadites. They were the ones who solved this caper!"

"And don't forget Devora's bad luck at dreidles," said Rebbe Doresh. "If she hadn't kept on getting a 'Shin' we might never have found the dot!" Everyone laughed.

"Speaking of dreidles," chimed in Chaim, "who wants to challenge the champ?"

"Okay, wiseguy," said Devora, "Set 'em up. I think my luck has changed now."

The Neighborhood Thief

evora stood in front of her house, her eyes reflecting both astonishment and worry. How, she wondered, could her parents' car still be sitting there, parked in the driveway? They had told her they'd be leaving no later than six-thirty, and here it was, after seven! Had something gone wrong?

She took the gift-wrapped package she'd been cradling in her arm and hugged it close to her body. Fumbling through her purse, she found her keys and opened the door just slightly. She peeked in, reassured herself that the hallway was deserted, and, brushing her coat along the side of the doorway, slipped inside.

She opened the closet door to her left and thrust the package inside. She made certain that the coats concealed the box and then closed the door.

Turning away from the closet, Devora was surprised to see a tall figure standing in the hallway.

"Sheldon," she cried, startled. "Is Mr. Weingarten still here?"

"Yes, he's just finished up his piano lesson with your brother. We started a little late today. I'm going to

warm up the car." Sheldon, Mr. Weingarten's sidekick
and assistant, hesitated for a moment, as if he wanted to
add something, and then abruptly walked out the door.

Devora entered the living room, and saw Chaim sitting at the piano, practicing his scales.

"You must practice more often," Mr. Weingarten,
his music teacher, admonished him. "It is not right for
your parents to spend money for your lessons if you
don't practice."

"But I don't like scales," Chaim wailed. "I want to
play the Hebrew songs that I know."

Devora's mother, sitting on the sofa reading, looked
up. "Oh, hello, Devora," she said to her daughter.
"Your father and I are a little late. But I'm glad you're
home now, to be with Chaim."

"So *that's* why you waited," Chaim grumbled.
"You're afraid to let me stay home alone. I'm not a
baby anymore."

Mrs. Doresh shook her head and sighed. "I know
that Chaim," she said. "But there have been a rash of
robberies in the neighborhood lately, and I'm a little
nervous. I'd rather the two of you be home together.
You can watch over each other."

"Gee," said Chaim, "Devora can't even watch over
herself. Look at her sleeve, it's filthy." He pointed to
Devora's sweater.

Devora looked at her sleeve and frowned. Some

gray putty seemed to have smeared on it. She rubbed it with her fingers, but it wouldn't come off.

"Okay, Chaim, what would you like to play?" asked Mr. Weingarten. Chaim mentioned the name of his favorite song, and Mr. Weingarten sat down at the piano and began to play it.

"That's beautiful," said Chaim. "That's what I'd like to play, not those boring scales."

"Ah, Chaim, those 'boring' scales will train your hands to do it. You've got to practice so that your fingers will be quick and stretch over the keys, like mine."

"Can you write down the notes for me?" The notes for the right hand, so that I can play it?"

"You have an ear for music, Chaim. Why not write them down yourself?"

"I don't have time for that," he answered, "but if you write them down for me, I promise to practice my scales every day."

Mr. Weingarten gazed at the flushed, eager face and gave Chaim's plump cheek a pinch. "You must practice because you want to play the piano. But all right, I'll write it down for you."

He glanced up at Mrs. Doresh, who was looking down at her watch and frowning slightly.

"Why don't you come to my house tomorrow and pick it up from me. I see that your parents are in a hurry, and so am I."

A car honked outside, impatiently.

"Mrs. Feldman was a little upset that you weren't going to Yossie's Bar Mitzvah tonight, Mr. Weingarten," said Mrs. Doresh, as she began to put on her coat.

"I'll tell you, Mrs. Doresh, these parties just end too late for an old man like me. Yossi knew his Bar Mitzvah *parsha* perfectly. He pronounced every letter correctly when he *lained*. That gave me more pleasure than any party could."

"Yes, Yossi was quite good," said Rabbi Doresh, who had joined them in the hallway. "I understand that you were the one who taught it to him."

Mr. Weingarten nodded his head in satisfaction and put his fingers back on Chaim's cheeks. "Soon I'll be teaching you your parsha, young man," he laughed.

"It's Parshas Vayera," said Chaim. Chaim had been dreaming about his Bar Mitzva since he had turned eight years old.

"Ah," answered Mr. Weingarten, "a musical parsha. You have the *shalshelet* there."

"The what?" asked Chaim.

"The shalshelet, a certain musical note used to emphasize a word. *Vayera* was my bar mitzva parsha too, that's why I remember it so well. The shalshelet was my favorite part."

Mr. Weingarten began to hum a strange little tune.

"Devora," Mrs. Doresh said, "make sure that you lock the door behind us. There's a draft coming in— you must have left it open when you came in."

Mrs. Doresh cut off Devora's protestations of innocence with a nod. "Just make certain it's locked."

Mr. Weingarten ended his tune and turned to leave. "See you tomorrow, boychik," he smiled at Chaim. "Good night everyone, and enjoy the party."

Devora followed everyone to the door. She watched Sheldon help Mr. Weingarten into the car and drive off. Her mother then joined Rabbi Doresh in their car, and they too rode off.

Devora turned to the door, and noticed a patch of gray paste stuck on the bolt. She saw an odd little metal disk in the middle of the sticky mess. Her fingers pulled on the disk and slipped it out of the lock. Strange, she thought absently, I wonder where that came from. She stepped inside and bolted the door.

"Chaim," she called, "come over here and give me a hand."

Devora opened the closet door and pulled out the package she'd put in just fifteen minutes before.

"What'cha doing, what's that?" asked Chaim.

"It's the present for Mommy and Abba. I expected them to gone when I got home."

"I kept telling them to leave," said Chaim, "but they wouldn't. Lucky you hid it in the closet."

"Well, help me find a place to hide it upstairs."

"Are you sure that they'll like it?"

"I know Mommy will. It's the perfect centerpiece for the table. I've been doing extra babysitting for this. She'll be very surprised."

"But it's an anniversary gift," protested Chaim. "It's for Abba too. Will he like it?"

"You should have seen Mommy's face when she saw it in the window. It'll make her so happy, that Abba will be happy too. But look, if you don't want to help pay for it, forget it . . ."

"Nah," Chaim said quickly, "it's all right. Besides, who wants to bother looking for something else. I have more important things to think about."

Later that evening, Devora looked up from her homework. Was that someone at the door? Perhaps Mommy and Abba had come home early?

"Who is it?" she called. But there was no answer.

It's only the wind, she thought to herself, and she turned back to her notebook with a shrug.

II

The next morning Devora looked out of her bedroom window and saw a police car standing in front of the Feldman's home, just three houses away. With a start she recognized her friend, Sergeant O'Malley, walking out of the car. She dressed quickly and flew out the door to find out what had happened.

She found her father, his tallis bag still in his hand, speaking with the sergeant. Rabbi Doresh turned to his daughter.

"Imagine that, Devora, they robbed the Feldmans last night, during their own son's bar mitzva! They cleaned them out."

Sergeant O'Malley nodded a greeting at Devora and flipped open his pad. "Did you hear or see anything unusual last night?" he asked.

"No," she answered. "Oh, wait—around nine-thirty I was doing my homework and I thought I heard someone at the door. I asked who it was, but no one answered, so I figured it was the wind."

"Nine-thirty. That's just when the crime occurred. The thief dropped a clock which stopped at nine-fifteen, so we're pretty sure of the time."

The sergeant frowned. "This is no simple case. It's not the first robbery we've had around here. We think that it's an 'inside job'—someone from your community. The burglar always seems to know when people are going to be out."

Rabbi Doresh frowned. "But if you think it was the burglar at my door last night, wouldn't he have known that my children were at home?"

"He couldn't have known," answered Devora.

"Chaim and I were invited, and we only decided a day before that we wouldn't go to the bar mitzva."

O'Malley studied Devora's face. "So you think it's an inside job, too?"

Devora ignored his question and asked, "How does the thief get inside? Aren't the locks bolted?"

"That's another strange thing," answered the sergeant. "The victims are all certain that they locked their doors, but when they returned they found the doors unlocked. And no one fiddled with the locks, our experts checked that. Here, take a look."

Devora and her father followed the policeman to the door. Rabbi Doresh grinned. "Looks clean to me," he said. The sergeant laughed but Devora looked thoughtful.

"Too clean," she said gravely. "In fact, this spot where the latch goes into the bolt lock is so shiny, it looks like it's been polished!"

The sergeant took another look and turned to Mrs. Feldman. "Has this been cleaned recently?" he asked.

"I really don't know. One of the children could have rubbed against it."

The sergeant turned to Devora. "She's right, it could have happened, but still, it does seem strange. But young lady, it's getting late and you should be going to school. Can I give you a ride in my squad car?"

"That's all right," answered Devora. "I usually meet my friends on the way to class. They're probably waiting for me."

She waved a cheerful goodbye and started off to school. She met a group of her friends, who were excitedly discussing the robbery.

"When our house was robbed," said Charne Saks, "we were at my sister's *sheva brochos*. My brother Kalman almost caught the thief red-handed, you know."

"How's that?" asked Devora.

"Well, Kalman had just finished his piano lesson with Mr. Weingarten. He really enjoys playing, and he begged my parents to let him stay home and practice a new song he'd learned. He said he was still tired from the wedding. But my parents insisted that he go with us. If he had stayed home, he'd have caught the thief in action!"

"How did the thief get in?" someone asked.

"The police think he walked right in through the door."

"He must be an expert locksmith."

"That's what the police said. It was a real smooth job."

The bell rang just as the girls walked through the door. The girls stopped talking and sat down for Morah Hartman's lecture on *Chumash*. The class was learning the story of the exodus from Egypt.

"One of the things that Moshe did before leaving was to get Yosef's bones," said Morah Hartman. "When Yosef died, the Egyptians wouldn't allow his bones to be brought to Israel. Instead, they placed his bones into a waterproof container and submerged it into the Nile. They hoped that it would bring good luck to all of Egypt."

"When it was time to leave, Serach, the daughter of Yaakov's son Asher, told Moshe where Yosef's bones were hidden. Serach had been promised long life by Yaakov, because she had told him that Yosef was still alive, so Serach had been alive when Yosef had died.

"Moses went to the Nile River and called out, 'Yosef, Yosef, we are prepared to leave Egypt. If you want to go with us, rise so that we can take you with us.'

"In answer to Moshe's words, Hashem made the container rise from the river and Moshe was able to bring the bones to burial in Israel."

The sound of the bell ended the lesson, and the girls hurried out to recess. A messenger from the office met Devora at the door with a note to call her mother at home.

"Don't come straight home after school," her mother told her. "Chaim is going to Mr. Weingarten's to pick up the musical notes that he wants, and I don't want him walking alone."

Devora smiled to herself. She could imagine Chaim's face when he found himself being "babied" like this. Still, she reflected, with a thief on the loose it wasn't a bad idea.

The burglaries were still on Devora's mind when she walked to Mr. Weingarten's house after school. Mr. Weingarten's helper Sheldon opened the door, and told her that Chaim was already with Mr. Weingarten in the living room.

As she walked towards the living room, Devora reviewed in her mind what she knew about Sheldon. He was very good to Mr. Weingarten, who had trouble with his legs and found walking difficult. Every afternoon Sheldon would go to Mr. Weingarten's house and drive him all over the neighborhood.

Sheldon loved tinkering with gadgets, and he had set up an intercom system all around Mr. Weingarten's house, as well as remote control buttons for the doors and windows. Sheldon was very handy and was always taking things apart and putting them together again.

Mr. Filipo in the hardware store had once told Devora that he didn't trust Sheldon. "It's something about his eyes," he had said. "Besides, he sometimes breaks things just so he can fix them, and I don't like that." Since then, Devora felt uncomfortable around Sheldon. She was glad when he showed her into the living room.

Mr. Weingarten was handing Chaim the sheets. "I wrote it out for you," he said. "Now, don't forget to practice the scales, like you promised."

"I will," said Chaim, who was more interested in a train set sitting on the table. Mr. Weingarten noticed his admiring gaze.

"Sheldon found this set in the garbage and fixed it for me," he said. "I always wanted a train set when I was a boy. Too bad I had to wait until I got old to get one."

"Oh, you're not *that* old," said Chaim, as Devora nudged him to silence.

"Sheldon can drive you home," offered Mr. Weingarten.

"It's all right," said Devora, "I have to do some shopping before we go home. Thanks anyway."

Mr. Weingarten noticed Chaim still eyeing the train set. "I know something you would love to see," he said, and he called Sheldon from the kitchen.

"Sheldon, I'd like to show these two my music room. Have you seen the key?"

Sheldon bit his lip and looked around. "I misplaced my key, and gave in the second to make a copy. We'll probably get it tomorrow. Besides, the piano there is no good. It has to be tuned."

"Why is this the first time that I'm hearing about this? What's wrong with the piano?"

"I'll work on it tomorrow. I've been busy with other things lately. As a matter of fact, Mr. Weingarten, I'm not sure how to tell you this. I think I'm going away tomorrow."

"Going away? Where?"

"California. I've been accepted in a university there."

"Mazel tov! I'm glad for you Sheldon, but I wish that you'd have told me about this earlier."

"I just got the formal notice today. I figured I'd tell you tonight, after the Mandelbaum lesson. It's getting late, we'd better start off to the Mandelbaums soon. They asked you to come early. They're going to a banquet tonight."

Mr. Weingarten looked unhappy. "I think I'll cancel the lesson tonight. I want to spend some time with you."

"Oh no, it's really not necessary. I can sleep over tonight, if you like. I'll buy dinner, and we can talk the whole night long."

"But what about your parents?"

"I told them already and they understand that I'd like to spend my last evening with you. Let's go to the Mandelbaums and then come back here."

"Okay," said Mr. Weingarten. "Come on, Devora, let me drop you and your brother at the grocery.

Chaim sat up front with Sheldon and Devora joined Mr. Weingarten in the back. Chaim shouted with delight when he saw the garage door open by remote control.

"It's a new world," sighed Mr. Weingarten, "a new world."

Mr. Weingarten lit up a cigarette. Devora turned away because the smoke always hurt her eyes. Mr. Weingarten noticed her discomfort, apologized, and opened the ashtray to put it out. He frowned.

"Where'd this napkin come from?" he muttered. "There's no room in the ashtray for my cigarette."

"Put the napkin in my lunch bag," Devora said quietly, eyeing the napkin. "I'll throw it away when I get home." Mr. Weingarten thanked her and threw the napkin in her bag.

She and Chaim finished shopping and walked home, discussing the surprise anniversary party which they were planning for the following evening.

"You're sure you haven't told Abba anything?" asked Devora.

"Sure, I'm sure. Are you positive that Mommy didn't find the box?"

"Yep," she answered. "I can't wait to see her face when she opens it," she added happily.

"Hey look, there's a police car in front of our

house," shouted Chaim, as they turned up their street.

"Maybe we've been robbed," he cried, as they both broke into a run.

Sergeant O'Malley was waiting for them and smiling. "Calm down, kids, nothing's happened. I just wanted to drop off the list of names of people who've been robbed. Maybe you can find some 'common denominator.'"

Devora eagerly scanned the list. There were the Feldmans, and the Saks. She also recognized Chaim's friends the Fuchs and the Adlers. Shaindy Nussbaum's parents had been robbed of antiques which had been in the family for generations.

"Okay," she said. "Thanks. I'll see if I can figure something out."

In the house at the supper table Mrs. Doresh spoke about the Feldman robbery.

"People are afraid to go out," she said. "I think the Buxbaum affair tonight will be the last for a long time in this community. The sergeant got a list of all the people that Rose Buxbaum invited and has promised to keep an eye on all of their houses. After all, the dinner honoring her and her husband will be in Manhattan."

"Are you going?" asked Chaim.

"I have to give a shiur tonight and your mother is tired from last night's bar mitzvah," answered Rabbi Doresh. "She's staying home this evening and will probably go to bed early. After all, mothers need their sleep too."

After supper Devora went up to her room to study. Opening her briefcase to get a pen she noticed her lunch bag and remembered the napkin Mr. Weingarten had found in the car. She took it out and studied it thoughtfully. Then she walked over to the chair where she had placed her sweater and examined the sleeve. Her eyes travelled from the sleeve to the napkin.

Devora frowned. She had never been in Sheldon's car and yet the gray pasty matter on her sweater looked the same stuff that was on the napkin.

I really must get my mind off these burglaries and get to work, she thought to herself. She opened her Chumash and began to review what she'd learned about Yosef's bones. Suddenly she frowned.

Devora left her room and headed back for the kitchen. Chaim looked up from his glass of milk and asked, "What's up? You look awfully serious."

"Where's Mommy?"

"In bed. I hope she won't be sick tomorrow. I'd hate to have to put off the party."

Devora walked over to the telephone. "Sergeant O'Malley please," she said. Her face fell. "Could you please tell him that Devora Doresh called and he should meet me at Mr. Weingarten's house. Thank you."

She hung up and looked at Chaim.

"You're going out now?" he said. "Mommy won't like it."

"It's important. And I'll leave her a note."

"Well, you shouldn't go alone. I'm coming with you. But maybe you ought to let Mr. Weingarten know that you're coming."

She dialed and listened to the phone ring. No answer.

"We'd better hurry," Devora said. "I hope that Sergeant O'Malley gets there quickly."

They boarded a passing bus and in ten minutes were standing at Mr. Weingarten's door. Devora rang the doorbell and waited. It was Sheldon who opened the door.

"What do you want?" he asked.

Devora was taken aback. "I . . . I want to ask Mr. Weingarten something. I'd like to borrow a record from him."

"Come in. I think he's sleeping." He left them waiting nervously in the hallway, but returned in a few moments.

"He's sleeping," he said. "What record do you want?"

"Forget it," she shrugged. "I'll ask him tomorrow. Uh . . . How come you have your coat on? I thought that you and Mr. Weingarten were going to spend the night together!"

Sheldon gave a short laugh and rubbed his hands

together. "You're a clever girl, Devora Doresh, but I am smarter than you. You'd better come here with me." He pushed her against the wall, grabbed Chaim's arm and twisted it behind his back. Then he flicked open a switchblade which he took out of a back pocket and held it close to Chaim's throat.

"Don't bother screaming, the old man is sound asleep. I put something in his food tonight to make sure of that," he grinned. "I've been packing the stuff that I stole into the car. Tonight I'll stop by the Buxbaums, pick up a few more things and check out. Then, I'm leaving the country with all the loot I've stolen in the past few months."

Sheldon led the two of them through the house. He opened a door and motioned for them to enter. "The music room," Devora murmured.

"That's right. A soundproof room. Mr. Weingarten never uses it in the winter, he says it's too cold. The perfect place to hide my loot. When he asked me for the key I knew it was time for me to leave town. Otherwise he'd keep asking me and get suspicious. I'm going to clean out the Buxbaums and be on my way. Mr. Weingarten will wake up tomorrow and won't be the wiser. And as for you, detective girl, I'll leave you in this soundproof room. Whenever Mr. Weingarten decides to come in . . . well, you'll be here to greet him."

He slammed the door behind him.

Chaim looked around and whistled. "So Sheldon is the thief. But what do we do now?"

"Don't worry, Chaim. I left a note and explained."

"How did you know that he was the thief?"

"I had no evidence, but I was pretty sure. I even think I know how he did it. Remember that gray gook I had on my sleeve? That proves that Sheldon was going to rob our house, too. He didn't realize that we had decided to stay home. And when he heard my voice, he slipped away."

"But how did he do it?"

Devora smiled and walked over to the grand piano in the center of the room. She saw a piece of paper underneath it, picked it up and carefully studied the notes written on it.

"What are you doing?" asked Chaim.

She began to play.

"Hey, isn't that the shalshelet tune?" Chaim cried. Suddenly the doors began to open.

"Let's go," she shouted to her brother, and they both dashed to the door.

They rushed to Mr. Weingarten's bedroom, and found him still sleeping soundly. Before Devora could get to a telephone, the doorbell rang. Chaim opened the door and saw Sergeant O'Malley.

"Sergeant," called Devora, "Mr. Weingarten's helper Sheldon is the thief. He's robbing the Buxbaum's right now!" The sergeant looked at Devora's face, then ran to his car and radioed his headquarters.

III

When Devora came down for breakfast the next morning, she found Sergeant O'Malley waiting for her.

"Well, Devora," he said, "all the stolen property has been recovered and I think that the victims want to give you a reward. You certainly deserve one."

Devora blushed.

"So tell me," the Sergeant continued, "how did you figure it out?"

"I couldn't figure out why I'd found gray putty on my door and on a napkin in Sheldon's car. Seeing all the gadgets in Mr. Weingarten's house, though, made me start thinking of remote control. What if the metal disk that I'd found in the door somehow could open the lock. But how? And then I thought of Yosef's bones!"

"Yosef's bones?" The police officer looked puzzled.

"It's something that we learned in school yesterday, about how a miracle took place when Moses said certain words. That, of course, was a miracle, but it made me start thinking. I've heard of toys that were voice-controlled that are being sold now—why not a voice controlled gadget to open a lock?"

"Sheldon was very clever. He always went with

Mr. Weingarten to the piano lessons. He knew when people were having simchas, and would schedule a late afternoon lesson for that day. He would go to 'warm up the car' and place a small disk by the latch bolt. He used the gray putty to hold it in."

"In the evening he would return. The disk was actually created like a record disk, with a special tune. All he had to do was play the tune on a remote control object which he carried with him. The tune on the disk would release the latch and the door would open! It's called a sound-activated switch."

"Yes," added Sergeant O'Malley. "Scientists today use it to translate sound into something mechanical."

"That Sheldon was a clever boy," said Rabbi Doresh. "What a pity he didn't use his brains for good things."

"I know someone who uses her brains to help people," said the Sergeant with-a grin. "And I think some of the victims would like to take her out to a restaurant tonight to celebrate the capture of the neighborhood thief."

"Tonight?" said Devora, with a secret glance at her brother. "No, thanks, Sergeant, but tonight I think I'd like a quiet evening at home. Right, Chaim?"

"Right."

The Case of
the Missing Ring

What a lovely wedding," murmured Mrs. Doresh, as she slipped into the car.

"Well, Rivka is the Kahaneman's only daughter, and they wanted everything to be just perfect," Devora said.

Chaim unbuttoned his dark blue vest. "Boy, those cigars Mr. Kahaneman was smoking smelled awful! I couldn't stand being next to him!"

Rabbi Doresh chuckled and started the car. "How could you smell anything, with that cold of yours, Chaim?"

Mrs. Doresh turned around and looked at Chaim, annoyed. "How many times have I told you to take tissues or a handkerchief with you? It's not nice to go around without one, particularly when you have a cold."

She opened the glove compartment and pulled out a box of tissues. "Here," she said, "blow your nose."

Devora laughed as Chaim leaned over to take a tissue. "We heard you sniffing all the way in the women's section."

Chaim growled but made no reply. Mrs. Doresh hastily changed the subject.

"Will you be meeting Regina tomorrow?" she asked Devora.

"Sure," said Devora. "*Ona khoroshaya studenka.* That's 'she's a very good student' in Russian," she ended with a smile.

Rabbi Doresh grinned. "Rabbi Margulies told me that you girls are doing a marvelous job with your classmates from Russia. The program to let the students teach them English was a very good idea. Sometimes students learn better from other students."

"Regina is very conscientious and I really enjoy learning with her. And she's teaching me quite a bit, too."

"Yeah," mumbled Chaim, "now the girls sit together and gossip in Russian."

Mrs. Doresh laughed. She was very proud of her daughter's work. There had been an influx of Russian immigrants into Kensington, a neighborhood not far from the Doresh's own. At first the *yeshivot* in the area were reluctant to take in students with such limited Jewish backgrounds. The principals had met and discussed the problem, and it was finally decided that each school would take in a specific number of students and try to incorporate them into the *yeshiva* system.

In Yocheved High, Devora's school, Rabbi Margulies had suggested that the students help the Russian girls until they were ready for the regular curriculum. Devora worked daily with Regina Rubnich, and had gotten very friendly with the Russian girl. The Rubnichs had even visited the Doresh's for Shabbos.

"As a matter of fact," Rabbi Doresh continued, "Mr. Kahaneman was one of the leaders of those opposed to admitting the Russians, particularly to Yocheved High. He doesn't feel that a strong Jewish education is very important for a girl. He'd have been satisfied if they'd just taught her how to cook and sew. And since the new students are an additional strain on the school's finances, Mr. Kahaneman was strongly against it."

"Boy, did you see Mrs. Kahaneman's jewelry?" Chaim said, between sneezes.

"She almost outshone the bride," replied his sister. "I'm surprised, though, that you noticed it."

"Oh, I didn't, really. I overheard someone else talking about it. He said that Mr. Kahaneman had bought his wife a brand new ring, just for the wedding."

Rabbi Doresh parked the car and turned around to admire his family. "You are my jewels," he said quietly, "and I am very pleased with what I have."

Once in the house, the Doresh family got ready for

bed. They had a busy day ahead of them, for Mrs. Doresh had offered to make a *sheva brochos,* one of the seven parties which are held in honor of the bride and groom during the first week of marriage. She planned to make the *sheva brochos* in her home the very next evening.

Noticing her mother's worried frown as she spoke of the *sheva brochos,* Devora said, "Why don't you ask Mrs. Kahaneman to send over Nora tomorrow, to help you out?"

"Oh, you mean her cleaning woman? She's not working there any more. Mrs. Kahaneman was so upset! She left just two weeks before the wedding. Mrs. Kahaneman has a new woman working for her, a Russian by the name of Helena. She seemed pretty efficient to me when I met her, but Mrs. Kahaneman is still used to Nora. She'd been with them for years, and was practically a member of the family. She even had her own key, and would let herself in and start cleaning while Mrs. Kahaneman was asleep. But I wouldn't want to ask a housekeeper to come and help me. Don't worry, I'll manage."

Early the next morning, as Devora sat eating breakfast, she heard the door slam shut. Chaim ran in, gasping for breath.

"Devora," he cried, "there's been a robbery at the Kahaneman's!"

"What?" she exclaimed. "How do you know? Who told you?"

"I passed by their house this morning, on the way back from *shul*. Sergeant O'Malley was there. He saw me, and he told me to tell you to come over there, if you had a chance."

Devora looked up at the clock. It was almost nine o'clock. She could rush over there, speak to the police officer, and still make it to class on time—if she was lucky. She *benched*, picked up her books and sweater, and hurried out towards the Kahaneman house.

Sergeant O'Malley stood in front of the imposing home, speaking on his car radio. A large crowd had gathered in front of the building and were excitedly discussing the robbery. When the sergeant saw Devora he switched off the radio and signalled her to follow him into the house.

It was the first time that Devora had ever been in the Kahaneman's house. Although she knew that the Kahanemans were one of the most prosperous families in the neighborhood, she was shocked at the lavishness of the furnishings. The sergeant lead her into a plushly carpeted living room. Devora silently noted the heavy brocade drapes, the many silver pieces gleaming from behind the window of a large display case, the sparkling crystal chandelier.

Mrs. Kahaneman's accusing voice broke through her

reverie. "Thief!" she cried, pointing an accusing finger at a small woman who was quietly crying in a corner of the living room.

"Please, Mrs. Kahaneman, we'll find the thief," said the sergeant. He turned to Devora and thanked her for coming.

"It seems to be an open-and-shut case," he said to her, "but I figured if my friendly neighborhood detective lives practically next door, I might as well call her in. Besides," he said with a laugh, "I know that you love being at the 'scene of the crime.'"

"What happened?" asked Devora, returning the sergeant's smile.

"Last night the Kahaneman's daughter was married."

"I know. I was at the wedding."

"Mr. Kahaneman had taken out a good deal of valuable jewelry from the safe deposit box where it is normally kept, so that Mrs. Kahaneman could wear it to the wedding. When they got home last night, they put all the jewelry into this box, and put the box on his desk. He planned on bringing it back to the vault today."

O'Malley turned to the police officer who was quietly standing next to Mrs. Kahaneman. "Have you checked the box for prints yet?" he asked.

"Yeah, Sarge," answered the officer. "The only fingerprints on the box are Mr. and Mrs. Kahaneman's."

The sergeant opened the box and Devora looked inside. She saw the lovely jewelry which Mrs. Kahaneman had worn the night before, sparkling and glistening in the black velvet-lined box. There was a bracelet heavy with rubies, an pair of diamond earrings and a matching diamond hair pin, a cocktail ring and a gold wedding band.

"The thief took only one piece, a ring."

"What kind of ring?" asked Devora.

Mrs. Kahaneman stepped forward. "The ring which my husband had bought me especially for the wedding. It was brand new. I had only worn it last night. Helena," and she looked meaningfully at the crying woman, "knew that it wasn't insured by us yet. My husband had planned to insure it this week. And that woman stole it, before he had the chance!"

"No, no!" Helena cried out, "I would not steal. I am not a thief!"

"Who else could have taken it?" snapped Mrs. Kahaneman.

O'Malley looked at his notepad, and continued speaking.

"Mrs. Kahaneman had given Helena the key to her house, so that she could come in without waking her and begin to clean up. Helena claims she walked in and went straight to the kitchen.

"When she woke up, Mrs. Kahaneman went down to her husband's desk to make certain that the jewelry was ready for her husband to take to the vault. She immediately saw that the ring was missing.

"As she walked towards the telephone to call her husband and ask him about the missing ring, she heard a voice in the kitchen, speaking to Helena. When she got to the kitchen she saw Helena handing something out the back door to someone, but she could not see who it was. It was then that she accused Helena of taking her ring and handing it to an accomplice."

The elderly woman wept openly. Devora noticed that she seemed frightened when the police officer spoke to her.

"You took my ring," said Mrs. Kahaneman again, pointing a manicured finger at the old woman. "Admit it, have it returned and get out of here. I won't press charges, but don't expect to get a job in this neighborhood again!"

Devora turned to the woman. "Please, Helena," she said gently, "why don't you tell us exactly what happened this morning."

"At seven-thirty I come to the house," she began, in accented and slightly broken English. "I know everyone will be sleeping, so I go to the kitchen to do my work. While I am working, I see Mrs. Kahaneman come down the stairs. Then I heard a knock on the door. It was my son. He had no money for the bus he takes to yeshiva so I gave him some money and he left. Then Mrs. Kahaneman walks in, screaming that I am a thief. I am not that kind of person!"

"Your son goes to yeshiva?" Devora asked quietly.

"In Russia, I could not teach my son how to be a Jew. But now that we come to America, I want him to be a good Jew. I go to classes at night and learn English, and he I send to yeshiva. I too would like to go to learn how to be Jewish, but there is no one to teach me."

"But of course there is," Devora broke in. "Why, right in this neighborhood there are classes that can teach you English and teach you how to be a good Jew at the same time!"

Helena stared at Devora. "You are a fine girl," she said. "I would like to go to these schools. But now all will think me a thief."

"Why didn't you tell us that it was your son who rang the doorbell when we asked you?" interrupted the sergeant.

"You frightened me. Mrs. Kahaneman frightened me. I was afraid for my son. But this girl, she make me feel that everything will be good."

"There is nothing to be afraid of," said Devora, trying to sound confident.

"So she's convinced you, too," said Mrs. Kahaneman bitterly. "Well, I've had enough of being a do-gooder, even if you haven't, Miss Doresh. These Russians! She has an answer for everything—well, Helena, how do you explain this?"

Mrs. Kahaneman whipped out a handkerchief which she'd been holding in her hand.

"What's that?" asked Devora.

"It's a handkerchief which we found right next to the jewelry box. And you'll notice the initial embroidered on it—an H. And," she added sarcastically, "I presume it doesn't stand for Peter Pan. No, Helena knew that the ring wasn't insured, grabbed it and handed it to someone waiting outside—her son, perhaps, or a friend."

Devora frowned. "No, that can't be right. There must be some other explanation . . ."

She broke off with a start and stared at the round-faced, heavy-set woman who had just burst into the room, despite the efforts of the police officer to keep her out.

"My friend Helena is not a thief," the woman shouted. "You all leave her alone!"

"And who are you, ma'am?" asked the sergeant.

"My name is Natasha. I am a friend of Helena. Believe me, sir, my friend is not guilty. She could not be, she is honest. Believe me, I know."

"Don't bother defending her, Natasha," said Mrs. Kahaneman. "It's perfectly obvious to everyone that Helena has done this to me. But her little game is up. Yes, the handwriting is on the wall for her and her thieving schemes."

"Handwriting is on the wall," murmured Devora, half to herself. "Wait—yes, that's it. It must be! *Mene Mene Takel Ufarsin!*" she shouted triumphantly.

"Huh?" said Sergeant O'Malley. "English, Devora, we speak English here, remember?"

"When Mrs. Kahaneman said that the handwriting is on the wall, she reminded me of a piece of Jewish history which we've just learned." She turned to Mrs. Kahaneman. "Do you know where that saying comes from?"

"Uh, no, no I don't. It's just one of those proverbs that we say."

"A Persian king by the name of Balshazzar once dared to use the utensils from the destroyed Temple during a party. So, we are told in the Book of Daniel, a strange hand came out of nowhere, and wrote down the words *Mene Mene Takel Ufarsin* on the wall. What it means, basically, is that you've been weighed and measured and found wanting. And that's the handwriting on the wall that everyone talks about!"

"Okay, Devora, that's a nice lesson in historical grafitti, but what does it have to do with this case?"

"Well, Sergeant, something has been bothering me about this. You see, Helena really couldn't have taken that ring. Mrs. Kahaneman, you admitted that she didn't plan the theft, because she couldn't know that you'd leave the jewelry out in the open, correct?"

"Well, yes, that's true," agreed Mrs. Kahaneman, reluctantly.

"Okay, so if it was done on the spur of the moment, if she just saw the ring and grabbed it, how could she have known that her son would be coming to the door? What would she have done with the ring? She would have known that she'd be suspected, and probably searched. It's not as if her son comes on a regular basis. And of course, since this wasn't planned, she couldn't have made up with an accomplice to come and get the ring!

"I began to think—if it wasn't Helena, it must have been someone else. But who? It had to be someone who could walk in and help herself to the ring."

"Whoever took it, dropped a handkerchief, and that handkerchief has a H on it. That sure seems to point to Helena," said Sergeant O'Malley.

"But don't you see, that's exactly what happened with the writing on the wall! The people at the party, you see, couldn't understand the language and didn't know what the words meant. They had to call in Daniel to interpret it for them. When Mrs. Kahaneman mentioned it, I began to think about language differences. And that's been our problem all along—a language problem. This whole problem then reminded me of the case of the Russian Connection. Remember that one, O'Malley?"

"I sure do. But where's the connection to this one?"

"Well, we can assume that this handkerchief does not belong to an American. It's a woman's handkerchief, you can tell from the lace at the edge. Americans, particularly American women, rarely carry handkerchiefs with them—they use tissues. My mother was just complaining about it.

"If it's not American, then it's probably foreign. And since there's been a huge influx of Russians in the neighborhood, I don't think it's too farfetched to figure that it belongs to a Russian."

"Aha! So that's even more proof against Helena. After all, she's Russian," said Mrs. Kahaneman.

"But don't you see? It's a language problem—a Russian language problem. In Russian the letter H is pronounced like our letter N.* So we're looking for a Russian who could get into the house, whose name begins with an N." And Devora looked significantly at Natasha.

The heavy set woman suddenly began to cry. "Yes, I

ˊАБВГДЕЕЖЗИЙКЛМНОПРСТУФХЦЧШЩЪЫЬЭЮЯ
абвгдеёжзийклмнопрстуфхцчшщъыьэюя

took the ring. Here it is," she said, and pulled out a gleaming gold ring from her pocketbook. "I came in here to say hello to Helena. She'd left the door open, but she must have been away, because no one was in the kitchen."

"Yes," said Helena, "I did go down to the basement for a broom."

"I went to look for her, and I saw a jewelry box. You know, things haven't been easy for us, and I needed the money, and I saw that there were so many other things, I thought it wouldn't be missed.

"I went down to the coffee shop on the next block, but I began to feel terrible about what I'd done. I don't need money that badly, to become a thief, I thought to myself. So I came back here, to return the ring. Only I found you accusing my friend Helena of my crime. I'm so sorry!" she sobbed.

"Here is your ring," she cried, and she thrust her hand towards Mrs. Kahaneman.

"Well, Mrs. Kahaneman," said Sergeant O'Malley, "you said you wouldn't press charges if you'd get your property back. You've got your ring, and it seems that Natasha won't try any more jewel thefts for quite a while!"

"Oh, I suppose there's no reason to press charges. There, there, quiet down," she said to the sobbing woman.

The sergeant turned to Helena, who was sitting quietly in the corner. "Helena," he said, "I believe I owe you an apology. I honestly believed that you had stolen that ring."

"Uh, yes, Helena, I guess I owe you an even greater apology," Mrs. Kahaneman added. "You know, I never realized how difficult it is for you immigrants to work, get an education, and give your children the opportunities they deserve. As part of your salary I'd be glad to pay for your son's tuition. And maybe you could use a raise—that is, if you'd be willing to stay on here and work for us."

Helena happily nodded her head. "I have no hard feelings, Mrs. Kahaneman. We all make mistakes."

"Not all of us, Helena. I know one detective who *never* makes a mistake." And Sergeant O'Malley looked at Devora.

Devora blushed and looked at her watch. "Oh, my! It's way after nine! I'd better rush, or the handwriting on *my* wall will spell trouble, in any language."

Everyone laughed as she ran out to school.

Message From Tangiers

It was the morning after Succos. The dim glow of dawn scattered the darkness and the shadows of dusk faded away. The rosy blush of the sun streamed through the window and shone on the figure lying underneath the blanket. Devora pushed her head out from underneath the covers and blinked her eyes. Was it morning already? She knew she was entitled to an extra hour of sleep . . . the school permitted the girls to come an hour later the morning after a holiday. The administrator realized that the girls would probably be helping their parents to clean up after the Yom Tov and since the holiday ended so late at night, it was necessary to ring the school bell an hour later than usual the following morning.

Devora stretched her body into a wide yawn and looked around her room. She had permission to go to the children's home that morning. During Chol HaMoed she had begun a project with some of the children in the home. They were making rings out of the strands from the Lulavim and the children loved doing it. Rabbi Sofer, who owned the Hebrew Book Store, had told her to come to the store the morning after Succos and he would give Devora his left over Lulavim.

She wanted to make rings, necklaces and bracelets with the children and this was a golden opportunity.

She said the Modeh Ani, washed her hands and looked into her mirror. "Devora Doresh," she whispered to herself, "it's getting quiet around here." For the past few weeks no mystery had knocked on her door. There was a gentle tap on her door. "It's me, Chaim," whispered her brother. "You told me to wake you early. I'm leaving for Shul now, so I hope you're up."

Devora put on her duster and opened the door. Chaim was startled to see her up. "Are you getting Lulavim?" he asked sheepishly. "I'd like to keep two for myself," he added.

"Sure, but what for?" she inquired.

"The Lulav is in the shape of a sword and although it's only October, we'll be having a Chanukah play in December and I'd like to use a Lulav-sword for my costume."

Devora sighed and nodded her head. Sometimes brothers could come up with the strangest ideas.

She dressed quickly, slipping into the school uniform blouse which matched a navy skirt, and brushed her thick dark hair—50 strokes. She checked herself again in the mirror, wrinkled her nose at a small pimple forming on her left lower chin, and walked out of her room. In the dining room, she davened and then entered the kitchen for breakfast which she took herself.

When she finally left the house, she locked the door and walked to Rabbi Sofer, but Rabbi Sofer's Hebrew Book Store wasn't open. Devora realized that she had forgotten that he wouldn't open before 10:30 so that even though school was extended an hour to open at 10:00, her plans for the day had changed. She frowned as she stood near the locked door and looked helplessly down Drori Avenue where she was standing.

The street was lined with stores—all kinds of shops whose metal gates were still drawn shut to keep intruders out. Hochberg's grocery was open on the corner and the hub of people going in and out of the store with bags of food gave life to the otherwise quiet street. There was Kova-hats, Beged-clothes, Mercava-Cars, Na'alos-shoes—the names of the stores were the Hebrew names for what they sold. . . . Even the fact that Rabbi Sofer sold Seforim or Hebrew books. "I guess everything has its sign," she mused to herself as she started walking toward Yocheved High. She stopped and looked at the window of Margolit-Jewels and admired a necklace that she had seen the day before, when she had met Shaindy and the two were walking together to visit someone who lived on Drori Avenue on top of the store.

"Devora Doresh," someone called suddenly. It was a voice she was familiar with from previous encounters.

The police car stopped and the driver waved to her, signalling for her to cross the avenue and come towards him.

"Hi, Devora, how come you're not in school today?" Lieutenant O'Malley fixed his eyes on the big clock hanging in front of the bank. "Don't tell me you're playing hooky!"

"It's *Isru Chag*," chuckled Devora. "The morning after a holiday school starts later. I was hoping the bookstore would be open but I'm afraid Rabbi Sofer also has an *Isru Chag*."

O'Malley's face then turned serious. "Do you have a moment, then? I'd like to ask you something."

She moved away from the car door as he pushed it open and heaved himself out. "I was on my way to speak to your father but maybe you can give me an opinion."

He stuck his hand into his jacket inside pocket and brought out a folded yellow manila envelope. He looked around the avenue at the traffic that was beginning to fill the street and then replaced the envelope again and stared at her. "Let's go to your house . . . I'll be there in a few minutes . . . I have to check something out first, okay?" He opened his car door and in a minute was on his way down the street in the direction of the precinct. Devora looked surprised by his action

but then shrugged her shoulders and started walking towards home.

O'Malley arrived in a few minutes after her. Her father wasn't home, and her mother was about to leave. "Don't be late for school," she warned Devora as she started walking down the street. Devora waited outside for O'Malley to drive up.

When he got out of the car this time, she realized that there was someone else in the car besides O'Malley. O'Malley did not introduce the stranger, but merely handed Devora the manila envelope and told her to open it. Devora emptied the contents of the envelope into her hand.

A single palm leaf rolled onto her fingers. She unrolled it and held it straight in her hand, then turned it over and examined it. Finally she shook her head and turned once again towards the Lieutenant. "I don't get it. This is a leaf of a Lulav . . . I've been making rings out of this material all week. Why are you bringing me one?"

"In my religion," explained O'Malley, "the palm leaf is used right before Easter. Have you ever heard of Palm Sunday?"

"But your Easter is around the same time we have Passover and that's in April!"

"Correct," announced the man from inside the car. He stepped out of the vehicle and stared at Devora. He was in his early thirties, about average height, stoutly built, jet black hair combed flat on his head, a double chin, and thick lips kept wet by a nervous habit of moistening them with his lips. "But you Jews use it *now*, don't you?"

Devora felt a dislike towards this intruder. "What did you call it, a LuLu?" He smirked as he said the word.

"Lulav," she corrected him. "On the holiday of Succos we use a Lulav."

"And you shake it, don'tcha?"

"We move the Lulav in six directions to show that Hashem rules over all directions of life—front, back, right side, left side, up and down."

"Well, our man in Tangiers is no Jew." He pronounced every syllable slowly and carefully.

"Please," intervened O'Malley, "Let me handle it. I wouldn't have allowed you to come along if I knew you would be antagonistic." The man wet his lips and looked ready to say something but then he decided not to, and shrugged his shoulders in compliance. O'Malley now turned to Devora and began to explain about the Lulav leaf.

"Our government has a plant in a North African country near Tangiers."

"A plant?" Devora wrinkled her nose as she looked at the leaf ... "What kind of a plant—palms?" The stranger snorted, "This is idiotic. I don't know why I listened to you," he insisted.

"I mean a plant . . . a mole . . . a spy for our government," explained O'Malley. "Trouble has been brewing in that part of the world. We've been ready for a coup for weeks now. A coup is a rebellion. It is in our interest to thwart the coup by informing the present pro-American ruler when it will take place. Well, we only have minimum information."

"Do you think the information was sent on the Lulav? Is it a microfilm?" asked Devora, trying to concentrate on what O'Malley was saying.

O'Malley smiled and looked at the stranger. "Heh, I told she's a smart cooky." He winked at Devora. "We checked it already. It's no microfilm," he continued. "Joe . . . Joe Taylor . . . he's our man. Every week he would send Izzy Schneider a letter . . . you know, a friendly letter. But it was coded and Izzy always understood the code. The agency encourages men to have trustworthy friends. More than one, though, is discouraged. So Joe and Izzy were buddies. Anyway, last month Joe sent Izzy the message about the coup and he explained that he'd send some prearranged signal about the coup . . . or when it would take place. . . . But we've gotta be sure that we understand his signal."

"I don't understand," said Devora thoughtfully. "Doesn't Izzy know?"

"Sure," O'Malley looked at the stranger and then at Devora. "Izzy knows except Izzy is out. He got hurt last week in a car crash. He's in a coma and a message came in from Tangiers. Now who's gonna figure it out."

"What do you want the message to tell you?"

"Whether we should go in next Tuesday. You see, when we go in, we bring Joe Taylor back with us, and his cover will be blown. That's why we have to be sure of the message."

"And that's the whole message . . . A Lulav Leaf?" She raised an eyebrow. O'Malley turned to the stranger again who was now staring at Devora. The stranger then turned to O'Malley and nodded his head. "Show her. It can't harm."

O'Malley passed a second envelope to Devora. Opening it gently, Devora removed a picture of a group of people holding sticks and shouting.

"What's this?" she asked as she examined the faces.

"This also came with the Palm leaf."

"Is Joe Taylor in the picture?"

"He's right here," said O'Malley, pointing to a man standing to the left of the photo. This man also was waving a pointed stick, and shouting something to the photographer."

The picture was hazy but still certain features were discernible. Joe Taylor had a handlebar moustache which looked like it was starting to grey. His hair was clipped short and close which emphasized the big moustache even more. Devora looked carefully at his mouth. "What is he saying?" she asked.

"We've figured out that everyone is saying the same thing. We've had special experts examining the lips to see if anything could be ascertained but everyone agrees that there is nothing special there."

Devora frowned and looked again at O'Malley. "What kind of person is Joe Taylor?"

The stranger leaned against the side door of the car and pulled out a pipe. He pushed the pipe into a special pouch and drew the tobacco like a shovel. Then he lit a match . . . the flame flickered in front of her eyes, casting an assortment of shadows. "Well," he began as he inhaled momentarily. "Joe Taylor was a South African landowner. During one of those tragic war accidents his wife and daughter were killed. He became very bitter. Almost had a breakdown. Izzy Schneider was part of a Commission from the United States to the African countries. Somehow the two met and hit it off right away. Izzy Schneider was a good agent and Joe Taylor was a good mole."

"Did Joe Taylor have any other family? Brothers, sisters . . . what about his parents?"

"There was a rumor he had a brother who died

when he was a teen. That's about it. We know nothing of his parents. I think they came from Europe."

"And then they became friends."

"Very close friends. They almost read each others' minds. They're the only two I know who wrote each other faithfully every week. Schneider, who is Jewish, used to write some Hebrew words on top of his letters—the Hebrew date, they said."

Devora fidgeted and looked at her watch. She would now have to run to get to school on time. The stranger noticed her anxiety and signalled with his head to O'Malley. "Oh well, thanks anyway," and he climbed back into the car. O'Malley studied Devora's face. "It's possible that there is no special meaning in all this, but I believe that Joe Taylor sent Izzy Schneider this message for a reason and that reason was to tell us to go in and get him out . . . the coup is under way. But no one will do anything until it is proven."

"Joe Taylor's your friend?" asked Devora.

"Joe Taylor's wife's sister is my wife's close friend," he answered glumly.

"Well, if I think of anything, I'll call you."

O'Malley drove away and Devora ran to school.

She made it for the second bell, and the moment she sat down, Morah Hartman entered the classroom. "Welcome back," she smiled at everyone. . . . "The

Yomim Tovim are over and now the real work of our semester begins." Some students in the back began to groan but in seconds everyone was concentrating on the lesson. "Sometimes events occur that we do not understand. Yet we know that the signs are in front of us. We need only to read them properly. Let me give you an example. One morning a man came to the Lubavitcher Rebbe to ask him for some advice. He told the Rebbe of some previous incidences that had brought him up to his point. The Rebbe listened quietly and then asked: 'What is the meaning of the word that is spelled Bais Kuf Reish?' The man looked at the Rebbe and said, 'the word is Boker, meaning morning.' 'Fine,' said the Rebbe, 'but how can you be sure that these same letters don't mean Bakar, cattle, or Biker, visited?' The man agreed, 'I would define the word you want in the context of how you want it.' The Rebbe smiled and nodded.' That is your problem, too. It is a problem of understanding the signs to know how to read them. It is important for you to know how to read them so that you will know which action to take.'"

Devora liked the thought. She leaned back in her chair and reviewed the events of her morning. Her mind riveted to the message sent by Joe Taylor but her thoughts suddenly zigzagged back to Rabbi Sofer, her brother, and the Lulav rings she was planning on fashioning. When the bell rang, she remained in her seat, locked in her thoughts.

"Devora," asked Morah Hartman, "is anything wrong?"

Devora stared at the face in front of her. For the moment she forgot that she was sitting in class. She blushed and looked down and then the snip of a smile crossed her lips. "No," she said, "everything is Boruch Hashem fine."

After school she called O'Malley. "The lulav is the symbol of the sword of Hashem. In olden times people always raised a sword as a sign of victory. When the Jews used to come out of Shul on Succos, they would raise their Lulavim high as a sign of victory over the evils of life. Joe Taylor did the same. You may think that he was waving a stick, but he let Izzy Schneider know that he was waving a lulav . . . the symbol of victory."

O'Malley was pleased, but he persisted. "How can you be sure that Joe Taylor knew that Izzy Schneider would understand this?"

"A Taylor in Yiddish is a 'schneider.' It is possible that after his family was killed, Joe Taylor found his missing brother. They may have kept it a secret from everyone. They may have been brothers, but surely coreligionists. That's why there was never any rift between them and that's why they could confide in one another and trust each other and, in fact, be so extra sensitive to each other's thoughts. So, Joe Taylor was signalling his 'brother' that he had been successful in thwarting the planned coup. And he was signalling this message in a way that only Schneider could grasp—and to make certain he understood, he enclosed a lulav leaf with his picture. By avoiding words to that effect, he was protecting his sensitive position as a United States agent."

O'Malley couldn't wait to get off the telephone to pass the revealing information which now made sense to him. But before he did so, he awkwardly exclaimed, "Thanks, Chief . . . er . . . I mean Devora. We'll follow it up immediately."

Devora giggled with bemused pride as she replaced the telephone in its cradle.

GLOSSARY OF TERMS

abba — Father

bais — Second letter in the Hebrew alphabet

Bais Hamikdash — The Holy Temple

bentscher — A booklet or sheet containing the Grace After Meals

bentsching — The act of reciting Grace After Meals

bima — A large table in the synagogue upon which the Torah scrolls are placed during public readings

bochur — An unmarried man

boruch Hashem — "Thank G-d." Literally, "G-d is the source of blessing"

bracha — A blessing

chag sameach — "Happy Holiday"

challah — A specially-baked loaf of bread eaten on the Sabbath and on festivals

Chanukah — Holiday commemorating the Jewish victory over the Greeks during their occupation of Israel during the years 168 and 165 B.C.E. When the Jews recaptured the Holy Temple, which had been desecrated by the enemy, they found a very small amount of holy oil for lighting the candelabra which stood in the Temple. The oil was only enough to keep the fire going for one day but miraculously the lights continued burning for eight days, long enough for a fresh supply to be acquired. In commemoration of the miracle, Jews light candles on an 8-branch candelabra, celebrating each day of the miracle.

Chazal — Acronym for *"Chachomeinu Zichronom Levracha,"* "Our Sages Of Blessed Memory"

chumash (plural, *chumashim*)—The biblical book containing the Five Books of Moses; Genesis, Exodus, Leviticus, Numbers, and Deuteronomy

daven — To pray

dreidle — A spinning-top used in a special game played on Chanukah

geniza — Hidden texts and documents

Gimmel — The third letter in the Hebrew alphabet

Haneiros Hallalu — Literally: "These lights," the title of a special prayer recited upon the lighting of the candelabra on Chanukah

Hashem — Literally: "The Name," referring to G-d. Since Jews are for-
   bidden to pronounce G-d's name in vain, they refer to G-d as *Ha-*
   shem

havdalah — Literally: "Separation," the ceremony performed immediately
   after the Sabbath has ended, to separate between the holiness of the
   Sabbath day and the weekdays which follow

Hey — The fifth letter in the Hebrew alphabet

Isru Chag — The day following a holy festival

kashruth — The science of keeping kosher, eating only foods permitted by
   the Torah

ketuba — A Jewish marriage contract

Kuf — The 21st letter in the Hebrew alphabet

lain — The term used for describing the special method of reading from
   the Torah scrolls in the synagogue

latkes — A specially-cooked potato pancake customarily eaten on the holiday of Chanukah

lulav (plural: *Lulavim*)—Branch of a palm tree, used in the ceremonials of
   the festival of Succos

Maged David — Literally: "The shield of David," a six-pointed symbol
   known as the Star of David

Maoz Tzur — A liturgical prayer sung following the lighting ceremony
   on Chanukah

menora — Candelabra

mezuzah — A small roll of parchment on which are handwritten the
   Shema and the two biblical passages concerning the love for G-d
   and his Torah (Deuteronomy 6:4-9 and 11:13-21). The *mezuzah* as
   affixed onto the doorposts of a Jewish home.

mitzvah — A commandment from the Torah, or the observance of one

Modeh Ani — Title of a brief prayer recited by Jews upon waking up in
   the morning

morah — Teacher

Nun — The 14th letter in the Hebrew alphabet

parsha — A section of the Torah read on a particular Sabbath

Parsha Vayera — The fourth *Parsha* in the Book of Genesis

posul — Invalid

Reish — The 22nd letter in the Hebrew alphabet

sefarim — Books; usually referring to religious books

sefer torah — Scroll of Torah, from which biblical portions are read publicly in the synagogue

Shabbos — The Sabbath, the seventh day of the week (Saturday) during which Jews do not work but rather rest and celebrate the creation of the world by G-d and their historic exodus from Egyptian bondage more than 3,000 years ago.

shalshelet — A musical note chanted during the reading of the Torah.

shammas — The candle used to light the candelabra on Chanukah

shema — Title of the biblical passage proclaiming the oneness of G-d (Deuteronomy, 6:4)

sheva brachos — "Seven Blessings," referring to the seven special feast for a newlywed couple following the wedding ceremony

Shin — The 23rd letter in the Hebrew alphabet

Shoftim — The biblical book of "Judges"

shul — Synagogue

sifre torah — Plural for *sefer torah*

spa ceba — Russian for "Thank You"

Succos — A holiday commemorating G-d's protection of the Jewish people as they travelled through the Sinai desert after their redemption from Egyptian slavery. Special "huts" are constructed during this 8-day festival in which the Jew temporarily resides in remembrance of his sojourn in the desert under the direct guidance of G-d.

tallis — Prayer shawl

Torah — The Five Books of Moses and other holy writings and teachings which elaborate on them.

yeshiva — A Jewish school in which Torah is taught

yomim tovim — Jewish Holy Days

About the Author

Carol Korb Hubner, daughter of the late Rabbi Moshe Korb and Mrs. Devora (Korb) Gartenberg, was born and raised in Chicago, Ill. until her early teens when she moved to Brooklyn with her family. She pursued her higher education at Stern College for Women where she received her B.A.

Mrs. Hubner has been a member of the presidium of the National Council of Bnos Agudath Israel and editor of its weekly newsletter. As counselor and head counselor of Camp Bnos her reputation as a story teller became legendary.

Wife to Rabbi Ehud Hubner, who is involved in scholarly talmudic research, mother of four children, and Bais Yaacov teacher, Mrs. Hubner's avocation is writing stories for young adults.

Acknowledgements

I am grateful to many people without whose editorial assistance this fourth volume of the *Devora Doresh Mysteries* would still be on the planning board.

—Gershon Winkler for his many imaginative and insightful contributions, as well as for his constructive criticism and editing.

—The skillful team of editors at Judaica Press: Elinor Nauen, Bonnie Goldman, Karyn Cohen, Miriam Zakon and Marcia Gasman, under whose supervision this book has reached its final form.

Particularly, I wish to express my gratitude to Mr. Jack Goldman of Judaica Press whose faith, encouragement and invaluable guidance spurred the swift continuation of this series.

C.K.H.